Christmas with The Darcys

A PRIDE AND PREJUDICE VARIATION HOLIDAY ATHOLOGY

LUCY CADEAU   SAMANTHA BANKS   BELLE HARPER

Daisy Chain Publishing

Copyright © 2023 by Daisy Chain Publishing

All rights reserved.

No portion of this book may be reproduced in any form without written permission from the publisher or author, except as permitted by U.S. copyright law.

A Curious Christmas Circumstance

One

ELIZABETH

"Elizabeth Bennet, please come collect this child from under my feet!"

Mrs. Bennet was in the Longbourn kitchen, trying to assist their housekeeper, Mrs. Hill, as they prepared supper for Christmas Eve. This would be their first holiday together as a family since dear Lydia's untimely passing the summer before. Their mother seemed determined to avoid any trace of sadness, especially for the sake of Lydia's little daughter, Helena.

When Lydia and her husband George Wickham died in a carriage accident, it fell to Elizabeth to take on Helena's care. As Elizabeth was meant to marry Wendell Davis in the new year, it seemed only natural that Helena become Elizabeth's ward. Jane and Charles were expecting their first child in the spring, Mary moved to America the year before, and Kitty could not be trusted to tend to anyone but herself. Elizabeth welcomed the opportunity to care for her niece, whom she loved dearly.

Wendell, on the other hand, was still adjusting to the idea of being a father to another man's child.

Elizabeth was engaged in hanging garland with her father and could not get to the kitchen.

"Wendell, dear, could you find Helena before she drives mama mad?"

Wendell, who was reading a paper in the corner, looked up with disinterest. "I will be on the lookout for her. I am sure Mrs. Hill has matters well in hand."

Unfortunately, it became clear that Mrs. Hill did not. When Mrs. Bennet had recruited the housekeeper to assist her in the kitchen; they both ceased to pay attention to Helena. Suddenly, the door to the butler's pantry opened and Elizabeth turned to see a little girl with blond ringlets, a smudge of dirt on her cheek, and one of her shoes unaccounted for.

"Helena!" Elizabeth gasped as she set the garland on the floor. "Where is your shoe? And more importantly, where is your grandmama?"

Helena's big blue eyes filled with tears.

Elizabeth took the little girl by the hand and led her to a stool. She picked up her missing shoe from the floor and dusted it off, then took a brush from her pocket to slick down Helena's curls. She was just about to brush the dirt from Helena's cheek when Elizabeth turned to find her mother staring at her in horror.

"Where has that child been?" Mrs. Bennet exclaimed. "She is dirty! She needs to be washed! Elizabeth, I will not have her in the house on Christmas looking like that."

"I will take her to the nursery and wash her, mama. Do not worry yourself. Go help Mrs. Hill."

Elizabeth picked up the little girl and made her way toward the stairs.

"I sent Mrs. Hill to the dairy to fetch more cream for the pudding!" Mrs. Bennet called after her. "Helena, are you hungry? Do you want a biscuit?"

Helena nodded and smiled at her grandmother. In the meantime, Elizabeth took the little girl up to the nursery. It had been her father's den for many years. However, he moved his things downstairs to make room for the new nursery that Helena would share with Charles and Jane's baby when they visited Longbourn.

Elizabeth played with Helena while she scrubbed her, wiped her feet, changed her clothing, and brushed her hair. Once they were finished, she looked every bit the picture of a young girl ready for Christmas. Elizabeth was certain her mother would be pleased. She carried Helena back downstairs and found her father sitting by the fire, sipping a glass of port wine.

"Well, well, well," Mr. Bennet said as his daughter and granddaughter entered the room. "My favorite girls have returned."

"Helena looks beautiful, does she not?" Elizabeth asked. "Your grandmama is in the kitchen, love."

Helena ran off to her grandmother once again, leaving Elizabeth alone with her father for the first time in ages. She smiled at Mr. Bennet as he poured her her own glass of port.

"Mama sent Mrs. Hill all the way to the dairy to fetch the cream for the holiday pudding? Did she not remember to purchase it yesterday at the market?"

Mr. Bennet laughed.

"I daresay Mrs. Hill has her hands full tonight. I think we should join mama in the kitchen."

Elizabeth followed her father. When they arrived, she found Helena standing by the stove with her grandmother. Mrs. Hill had a bowl of pudding in her hands, but no sign of the cream. The housekeeper spread her hands out before her, as if to say there was nothing she could do.

"Mrs. Hill," Mrs. Bennet said, "tell your story again."

"Yes, ma'am." Mrs. Hill cleared her throat. "I went to the dairy to fetch the cream for your pudding, as you asked. As I was leaving the dairy, I ran directly into Mrs. Cole, the housekeeper at Netherfield. She informed me that Fitzwilliam Darcy has come to stay, and will be joining Mr. and Mrs. Bingley when they come to Longbourn tonight! "

Mrs. Bennet glared at her husband. "Did you know about Mr. Bennet?"

"I did not. I certainly would have mentioned it if I did."

Then she turned to Elizabeth, who certainly did not know Darcy was in Meryton. She had done well to avoid him for the last several years and did not wish to renew their acquaintance now... especially while Wendell was at Longbourn.

"Mama, if I knew Fitzwilliam Darcy was here, do you not think I would have told you?"

Mr. Bennet held up his hand. "I do not understand. What does that have to do with the cream for the pudding?"

"I told you." Mrs. Hill said. "I ran directly into Mrs. Cole and spilled the cream. The farmer had no more on hand."

Elizabeth picked up Helena before she could get her hands in the flour and make a mess of her clean dress. If Fitzwilliam Darcy was coming to Longbourn, it truly would be an unforgettable Christmas.

Two

DARCY

Fitzwilliam Darcy paced the study of Netherfield in frustration. Charles Bingley sipped a cup of tea without a care in the world as his friend traced a trail of his worry in the rug. He did not intend to trick Darcy when he invited his oldest friend to visit for holidays, but when his wife suggested they spend Christmas with his in-laws, he could not come up with a plausible reason to say no.

"Charles," Darcy said when he finally ceased pacing. "When I accepted your invitation to Meryton for the holiday, I did so under the assumption we would spend Christmas at your home. Not Longbourn. You know the Bennet family tires me. And there are so many of those Bennet girls!"

Jane appeared in the doorway and coughed lightly.

"As a matter of fact, the only sister still at Longbourn is Elizabeth, and that will not be the case much longer. There is plenty of space, which is why we will be staying at Longbourn tonight at mama's request."

Charles sighed with weariness.

"Oh, Jane. Why did you tell her we would stay? We could have simply seen them at church in Meryton tomorrow and spent the rest of the day here, as planned."

"I know, but we are going to be away for the next several months until the baby is born. I thought it would be nice to spend Christmas together."

"It would have been nicer if we could have spent it at Netherfield!" Fitzwilliam continued to complain as he returned to his pacing. "This means I will be forced to see Elizabeth again. You must remember, Charles, that I spent many months trying to attract her attentions during my first visit to Hertfordshire... but she would have none of it."

Charles shook his head at his friend's stubbornness. "I know, I know. But why does it matter now? You have been away from her for years!"

"It matters because she turned me down. It matters because she is one of the most vexing, obstinate girls I have ever met. It matters because I could not forget her after I left Hertfordshire. It matters because I have not been able to get her out of my mind."

"Fitzwilliam," Jane said as she took Darcy's arm in her own. "It will be a wonderful time, I assure you. And, most importantly, I need your assistance with the things we will take over to Longbourn. There are gifts for little Helena and a cake for dessert."

"You will have to ask your husband," Darcy said. "I have no intention of going with you."

Jane chastised him as you might a petulant child.

"Come now, Fitzy. Do you truly want to spend Christmas alone?"

"Yes! Alone. With only my thoughts and a nice glass of sherry."

Jane sighed in annoyance.

"You would not truly be alone if you stayed here regardless," Jane argued, knowing that her husband would not leave Darcy by himself for the night. "You would have the servants for company."

"Yes, I suppose I would," he said, prompting a chuckle from

Charles. "Very well. I will come. But no one will recognize me because I scowl forlornly the entire time I am there."

Charles laughed, but Jane was not so amused.

"How would that be any different than your usual appearance as of late, Fitzwilliam?" she asked. "Charlie, please tell your friend to cheer up. Mama is making her Christmas pudding and it is renowned far and wide. I promise, you will have a lovely holiday."

Darcy turned to Charles and crossed his arms over his chest. "What say you, old friend?"

"Well, I cannot guarantee a lovely holiday while my mother-in-law still lives at Longbourn," Charles said. "However, I think it is most important that we attend this year. For the sake of little Helena."

Jane smiled at her husband before taking her leave. After several moments, Charles cleared his throat.

"I should go assist Jane. Darcy, old chap, you need to discover a bit of the holiday spirit."

Once he was alone again, Fitzwilliam mumbled under his breath as he resumed his pacing.

"Holiday spirit, indeed."

Three

ELIZABETH

The Bennet family gathered in the drawing room as soon as they heard a carriage approach the house. Helena attempted to run to the door, but Elizabeth was able to catch her before she could escape. Charles and Jane stepped inside first, followed by Fitzwilliam Darcy. Elizabeth forced a polite smile, but was grateful she was able to hide behind Helena.

Mr. Bennet greeted him warmly, as if they were longtime acquaintances. Mrs. Bennet immediately began to coddle the handsome man, asking about his trip from Pemberley and if his sister had recovered from her illness. News of Georgiana Darcy's sudden and mysterious sickness had spread far and wide. According to Charles, however, she was convalescing in a hospital in Brighton and on the mend.

Wendell appeared by Elizabeth's side and gave her a fright.

"Did you know Darcy was going to be a guest here this Christmas?" her fiancé asked, his lips pursed. Elizabeth tried to maintain her smile thought it was becoming increasingly onerous.

"He had a very difficult year, Wendell. Please, be polite to him. If I can manage it, you can as well."

"But..."

Elizabeth did not allow Wendell to continue; instead, she put Helena down on the floor so she could assist her sister with her coat.

Mrs. Bennet was still chatting about Darcy's next visit to Brighton when Mrs. Hill appeared to announce dinner. Elizabeth breathed a sigh of relief as everyone headed toward the dining room. Helena practically ran on her chubby little legs to reach Darcy, much to everyone's surprise, as she rarely showed much interest in strangers.

"Well, hello little friend," Darcy said as he held out his arms. Helena hurried to him, nearly tripping over the man's feet. "Shall we take a walk?"

Helena giggled as Darcy carried her into the dining room and set her in his lap. Elizabeth followed them and sat by Darcy's side. Under normal circumstances, the little girl would have reached immediately for Elizabeth. Instead, she stayed with this mysterious stranger who was feeding her sugar cubes.

"Mr. Darcy, if she is bothering you, she can eat her supper in the kitchen with Mrs. Hill. I do not want to interrupt your meal."

Much to her surprise, the gentleman smiled and shook his head.

"She is quite a delight, Miss Bennet. She reminds me of Georgiana when she was a girl. Your sister did not tell me you had a child."

Elizabeth felt like she had the afternoon Kitty poured a bucket of cold river water over her head when they were children. The whole table turned and looked at Darcy in horror. He knew he had committed a grievous error, but clearly did not know what it was. Elizabeth felt compelled to take pity on him.

"I take it you did not hear of the passing of George Wickham and my sister, Lydia."

All of the color disappeared from his face.

"I had not. My condolences. To all of you. People tend to avoid talk of George Wickham where I am concerned. If I had known... My deepest apologies. Was she their child?"

Elizabeth nodded.

"Her name is Helena and I am her guardian. Well, my fiancé, Mr. Wendell Davis and I, will be her guardians upon our marriage. It has been a very eventful year."

Darcy cleared his throat and looked down at his plate.

"I could not imagine such sorrow. I am sorry."

All of the color slowly returned to the man's face as he looked at Elizabeth. For the first time since they met, she felt as though she was truly looking at him. He had grown up, matured somehow. The last time she saw him, he was so full of himself and his wealth. He was also angry with her for rejecting his advances.

Mr. Bennet cleared his throat, which reminded the two of the other guests at the table.

"Darcy, how is your sister?" her father asked.

"She is well. A family friend is currently staying with her in Brighton while I came to attend some business in Meryton. I am thankful you allowed me to spend the holidays with you."

Elizabeth noticed that Charles laughed when Darcy said that, and she made a note in her mind to ask him why later.

"Well!" Wendell said so suddenly he startled everyone. "Shall we eat? At last."

Christmas Eve dinner was served at Longbourn and while everyone ate with fervor and good cheer, Elizabeth could not help but wonder...

What had caused such a change in Fitzwilliam Darcy?

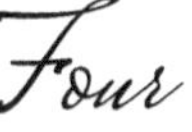

DARCY

When dinner was over, the household retired to the parlor to sing carols. Darcy was never one for singing, but the pleasant atmosphere in the Bennet home was improving his spirit by the moment. The fact that he held a sleeping Helena in his arms went a long way to softening his previously hardened heart.

He looked down at Helena, who stirred a little as he sat in a chair by the fire. In an attempt to prevent her from waking, Darcy sang his favorite carol, "God Rest Ye Merry Gentlemen," softly in her ear. It was not long before he realized everyone was looking at him.

"Goodness," Jane said with amazement. "I do not believe I have ever heard Mr. Darcy sing."

Charles and Elizabeth exchanged looks.

"It has been a very long time since I sang with anyone," Darcy confessed.

"What a shame! We shall have to remedy that," Mrs. Bennet said as she clapped and sat behind the piano. "Mr. Darcy, do you know 'Good King Wenceslas?'"

Darcy politely nodded, despite the fact that he rarely sang in front of anyone but family. However, Helena stirred again, this time opening her eyes to look about her.

"Shh," Darcy whispered to her. "Sleep, little one. Soon it will be Christmas."

Halfway through the song, Helen began to cry, only to be silenced when Darcy pressed a kiss to her head.

ELIZABETH

Elizabeth watched as Darcy held Helena and tried to figure out what it was that had changed in him. Ever since she rejected his marriage proposal, on the rare occasion they saw one another, he had been polite, but distant. Tonight, he seemed almost... free.

While Darcy held her niece and sang, it was almost as if Elizabeth was looking at a different man. He was clearly enjoying himself.

"I am exhausted, Lizzy," Wendell said when he appeared by Elizabeth's side. He kissed her on the cheek and suddenly, she felt the urge to move away. "I think I will retire for the evening."

It was still so early and the carol singing had only just started. Wendell always did this at parties; he left just when everyone else was beginning to have a pleasant time.

Elizabeth paused for a moment and took a deep breath. She had a strange feeling in her stomach; something between dread and curiosity. When she looked over at Darcy, she noticed how attentive he was to Helena.

"Have a pleasant night, Wendell. I will see you in the morning for Church."

"Very well," he said and continued on his way. He did not stop to say goodnight to her family.

As she approached Darcy and Helena, Elizabeth felt a nervousness she had not felt in a very long time. It was a strange sensation.

"You... you have changed."

"What?" Darcy looked up and Elizabeth suddenly realized what she had said.

"I only meant... you seem different tonight. I did not expect it."

He smiled as he looked down at Helena. "Nor did I. I suppose your niece has brought out a side of me I had long forgotten."

When the carol was finished, he gave Helena to Elizabeth, who in turn, took the child to her nursery where she could sleep for the rest of the night. Mrs. Bennet followed Elizabeth to help her change Helena into her night clothes.

"Mr. Darcy was very good with her," Elizabeth said as she pulled the blankets around the sleeping girl. "She is usually very wary of strangers."

"Do not be surprised if he renews his request for your hand in marriage," Mrs. Bennet said as folded Helena's little dress.

"Mama!" Elizabeth protested.

Helena stirred in her sleep and began to cry again.

"Calm down, sweet one. Aunt Lizzy is here," Elizabeth cooed. The little girl drifted back to sleep. Mrs. Bennet stood beside Elizabeth and shook her head.

"I had such high hopes that Mr. Davis might make a good father to Helena, and a good husband. But it is clear Darcy has taken a fancy to Helena. He has a natural instinct for children."

Elizabeth stifled a sigh. "Mama, do not be silly. I am engaged to Wendell. And just yesterday, if I had mentioned Mr. Darcy's name in this house, you would have forced me to sleep in the stable."

Mrs. Bennet shrugged as if she were merely making conversation.

"He seems to be a very good man, Lizzy. I understand why you turned him away once. But if he is still intent on making you his wife, I think you should consider his offer."

Elizabeth was silent. She did not want to think about this tonight. Not at Christmas. But if Darcy was still interested in her after all this time *and* he cared for Helena?

"Will you consider it?" Mrs. Bennet asked again as they left the nursery.

"Perhaps I should," Elizabeth said when they returned to the parlor, where the others still sang.

"Why are you being so agreeable, Lizzy? Are you trying to shock me?"

Elizabeth ignored her mother's playful smile. The night was young and there would be time for this later. For now... there were carols.

Six

DARCY

The Christmas candles had long been snuffed out and most of the household had retired for the evening. Fitzwilliam Darcy, however, found that he was unable to sleep. As the fire in the parlor was still burning, he poured himself a glass of port and sat down in the most comfortable chair. He was even starting to feel a bit drowsy when Elizabeth's fiancé, Wendell Davis, appeared out of the shadows. When he addressed him, Darcy was so taken aback that he almost dropped his glass of port.

"What the devil are you doing in here?"

Drunkenly, Davis staggered over to the fire and threw a log into it.

"Warming myself. It is Christmas," he said. "I am trying to enjoy myself."

Darcy was too surprised to reply at first. "You should be in bed, Mr. Davis."

Davis sat down in another chair and stared at the fire. When it was obvious that he was not going to leave, Darcy continued to sip his port and watched him as he did.

"So you are the one who tried to woo my fiancé," Davis said after a moment.

Darcy did not reply. They both just sat there, watching the firelight. The room was silent except for the crackling of the logs. Darcy took another sip of his port, then he set the glass down on the table beside him.

"I can assure you, Mr. Davis, I am not currently attempting to woo your fiancé."

He hoped that might be the end of the conversation, but then he noticed that the man's hands were shaking. Whatever was coming next, it was not going to be an amicable end to their meeting.

"What in God's name are you thinking?" Davis yelled suddenly and angrily. "You want to marry Elizabeth? Are you completely mad?"

Darcy frowned and stood up. "I would not ever presume to give you orders, Mr. Davis. However, I do believe you had better go to bed."

"No!" Davis shouted and crossed the room in two strides, so that he stood right in front of Darcy. "You know nothing. You have no idea of what you have done."

Darcy could feel his heart pounding in his chest. If the man was going to hit him, he would have to do it over his dead body.

"You are out of control, sir, and you are going to wake the whole household," he said, his voice surprisingly steady. "You should return to your room and sleep."

Davis grabbed Darcy by the collar and pushed him against the wall. At that moment, Darcy could see that the man was not only drunk, but furious. His hands were shaking and he was almost foaming at the mouth.

"Do you intend to ruin me, Darcy?"

The door opened, and all at once, half the household appeared. Elizabeth, standing in the front, looked as if she had been asleep, but her eyes were wide with alarm.

"Let him go, Wendell," Elizabeth said. Darcy could hear the concern in her voice.

"No," Davis said and pushed Darcy harder against the wall. "I will not let him go. Not until he admits that he is trying to destroy my life."

Elizabeth stepped forward and reached for Wendell's hands, trying to pry them from Darcy's collar. "I want you to let him go, Wendell."

"No! I will not do it," Davis replied and pushed her away. She fell backward, landing on the couch.

Darcy saw the servants exchange worried glances, but no one dared to intervene. Meanwhile, Davis was still holding him. And it was as if he had no intention of stopping until Darcy confessed to whatever it was he thought Darcy was doing to him.

"Mr. Davis, you are making a mistake. From what I can see, if Elizabeth decided to marry you, then you should consider yourself grateful, because you are hardly deserving of her. Now, unhand me, before you regret it."

"I am not grateful!" Davis shook him. "You want her for yourself. You want her to be your mistress."

Darcy had quite enough. He kicked Davis in the shin, and the man released his grip immediately. In one swift motion, Darcy had him on the floor and his arm against his throat.

"I have no idea what your problem is, Mr. Davis, but I suggest that you take the night to think about it," he hissed, his anger barely in check. Then he let him go and walked away.

He had nearly reached the door when Elizabeth's voice stopped him.

"Are you all right, Will?"

He turned to her and the expression on her face was full of concern.

"Of course, I'm all right," he said. "I was barely touched by that lunatic. Are *you* hurt at all? Do you need the doctor?"

She shook her head just as her sister and mother finally left the safety of the doorway.

"Elizabeth," Jane said as she wrapped her sister in a hug. "Do I need to wake Charles? He and father had too much wine and slept straight through that but if you want them to send Wendell away..."

Darcy stepped forward. "I would be happy to do so, if you wish." After what had just transpired, nothing would have brought him greater pleasure than to throw Wendell Davis onto the front steps of Longbourn. But Elizabeth refused.

"It is Christmas. Let us show him charity and revisit this in the morning."

While the ladies returned to bed, Darcy remained in front of the fire, finishing his port and considering what had just transpired. He may not have expected any of this when he left Netherfield, but it seemed it was time to change his plans...

Seven

Christmas morning came to Longbourn, and with it, a surprise blanketing of snow. Elizabeth woke early to dress Helena in her best gown. Even though she would not accompany them to church, she wanted the little girl to look splendid when the time came for Christmas lunch.

Even though word of Wendell's atrocious behavior from the night before would have spread, she hoped they could have a pleasant Christmas Day regardless. After all, it was a joyous occasion, and if they could get through today, then tomorrow was soon enough to confront her fiancé. She also hoped to speak to Fitzwilliam again before she made any rash decisions.

After breakfast, Elizabeth and her family were just about to leave for church when the whole party was brought to a stop Wendell's appearance in the foyer. She did not think he would dare show his face for the rest of the day, so it was quite a surprise to find him waiting for them at the front door.

"Wendell," Elizabeth said cautiously. "Good morning. Are you feeling better?"

He ignored her question and instead, he handed her a package of some sort. "This is for you," he said stiffly before turning on his heel.

"What's that?" Jane asked. Elizabeth looked at the package, then back at the door, but Wendell was already gone.

"I have no idea," Elizabeth said. "Should I open it now?"

Mrs. Bennet scoffed.

"Of course, you should!"

Elizabeth walked to the library, turning the package in her hands. She handed it to Jane and asked her to cut the strings that bound it together. They were all surprised to discover it was a book. The book itself was bound in dark leather, and it was heavy. Someone had obviously written their name on the cover, but the ink had smeared with time and it was very difficult to make out.

"It looks like a diary," Elizabeth said with a frown. "Have you ever seen it before?"

"I have not."

Jane handed it back to Elizabeth, who carefully opened the cover. After examining the cover under a light, she realized it was her sister Lydia's diary. Some of the pages were smudged, but she recognized the handwriting as Lydia's.

"Wendell must have found it in Lydia and Kitty's old room. I was sure she took all of her possessions with her when she left," Elizabeth said in surprise. "What a lovely discovery. We must save it for Helena."

Jane sighed thoughtfully. "It seems Wendell did one thoughtful thing before he departed. Little Helena will be able to know her mother after all."

Elizabeth opened the diary to the first page and gasped in surprise. She began to read and then to laugh, tears forming in her eyes. When she finished the first page, she simply handed Jane the diary and looked back at the door. The man who had just left had no idea what he had done.

"It seems you received the gift," Mr. Bennet said as he entered the room.

"Indeed," Elizabeth replied and returned to reading. "Helena is going to love it one day. I can't wait to show it to her."

ELIZABETH and her father were the last to arrive at church. The snow made the walk challenging, but Mr. Bennet had insisted on going. They were all bundled up against the cold and Elizabeth was grateful she did not have to go the whole distance on her own.

The service was long and the Reverend did not seem inclined to return to the parsonage. Halfway through, Elizabeth could think of nothing but returning to Longbourn so she could speak with Darcy, who stayed behind to entertain Helena. She wanted to know if there was any chance he still cared for her the way he once did.

But first, she needed to talk to her father.

When they returned, Elizabeth found her chance. She pulled her father aside and asked for a few minutes alone with him.

"It is about my future, Father. We must speak," she said. Mr. Bennet looked at her, analyzing her face, and then nodded.

"Very well."

When they were alone in the library, Elizabeth began to speak, but her father stopped her.

"Before you tell me anything, I need to tell you something of my own. I know."

Elizabeth reached out and took his hand.

"You do?"

He had heard everything the night before. Mrs. Bennet made sure to fill in the empty spaces on anything he missed. Much to her surprise, he was supportive of whatever she chose.

Mr. Bennet smiled at her. "I will not pretend that I cared for Wendell Davis, nor do I know much about Fitzwilliam Darcy. But if he will make you happy, then you have my blessing, for you and Helena."

Elizabeth gave her father a hug and then ran off in search of Fitzwilliam. She needed to know how he felt, and now, before Christmas Day was done.

Eight

DARCY

It was almost time for Christmas lunch, and Darcy knew that they would be departing for Netherfield soon after, so he wanted to spend as much time with Helena as he was able. There was something about spending this holiday with a big family, with little Helena, and Elizabeth, that made him feel joy for the first time in a very long while. He also found himself drawn to the little girl every time they were together.

He had never considered children until now, but if he was honest with himself, he wanted them. He wanted to raise a child that was as good and kind as Helena. And he knew that Elizabeth would be a wonderful mother, as she was already one to her niece. Darcy did not think it was possible before, but perhaps now... she would consider his offer once again.

He had been sitting happily in the nursery with Helena, reading her a book, when he heard a knock. He looked up, surprised, and he smiled. Elizabeth stood in the doorway, wearing a beautiful blue dress, her hair done up and her eyes sparkling. She was as bright as the snow.

"Elizabeth," he said and closed the book. "It's so good to see you."

She smiled and walked towards him. As she approached, he noticed that she appeared a little nervous. He stood and placed Helena with her toys. Elizabeth took his hands as soon as he was close enough.

"Fitzwilliam, you were right."

Darcy's brow furrowed and he looked at her with surprise. "Elizabeth, what do you mean?"

She looked up at him, her face beaming.

"I understand now what you tried to tell me all those years ago. And you were right. I believe we are meant to be together. I love you, my darling Fitzwilliam."

His heart swelled, and he could feel tears in his eyes. He had not dared hope this would happen. He reached up and brushed away her tears, his own eyes blurring.

"Elizabeth, you are the most beautiful woman in the world. You have my heart."

"And you have mine," she replied and leaned into him. They held each other close, their hearts beating as one.

"I have been so worried. I thought you were going to marry Wendell Davis. I thought I had lost you."

"No, you never have to worry about that," she said. "You are my only."

"And you will always be," he said with a kiss.

Helena toddled over and wrapped her arms around Darcy's legs, prompting him to lift her off the ground. He kissed Elizabeth and the little girl on both their heads. When he spoke, he could scarcely hide the joy in his voice.

"Well, it appears we have a lot to celebrate today."

"Indeed," Elizabeth said with a smile. "I wonder what my parents will have to say about this development."

"What development might that be?" asked a voice from the doorway.

The couple looked at each other and then laughed when Mr.

Bennet came into view. He walked over and took his grand-daughter into his arms.

"Papa, Fitzwilliam has a question to ask you."

Mr. Bennet laughed. "I suspect that you would like to ask for Elizabeth's hand in marriage?"

"Yes, sir," Darcy said and turned to Elizabeth. He looked at her in shock.

"Elizabeth, you told your father?"

"Yes," she said and smiled at him. "I did."

"What could I say?" Mr. Bennet shrugged. "I knew from the moment I saw you two together that you were meant to be."

Elizabeth and Darcy looked at one other and Darcy took her hands in his.

"Elizabeth, will you do me the honor of becoming my wife?"

Elizabeth leaned up and kissed him.

"Yes, Fitzwilliam. Yes."

They embraced and laughed. Mr. Bennet shook his head and smiled.

"Well, I can see I will have to get used to this sudden change in your relationship."

Darcy took her face in his hands. "Elizabeth, I love you. More than you know."

"And I love you, my darling Fitzwilliam."

He held her like he was never going to let her go.

ELIZABETH

By Christmas evening, Elizabeth was practically hoarse from telling the story of their engagement. Helena ran around the parlor with a sparkling grin on her face, so happy that everyone began to wonder if she knew what had transpired. Her little squeals of delight brought a smile to everyone's face, even Mrs. Bennet's.

Elizabeth and Darcy sat next to one another on the couch in the parlor, holding hands and staring into each other's eyes. They could not believe how deliriously happy they were. However, Elizabeth could not help but think their happiness came at Wendell's expense. Yes, he had behaved atrociously, but were it not for him, they may never have found Lydia's diary.

"Fitzwilliam," she said and looked at him. "I am worried about what will become of Wendell. He may not have been the best man, but he was not the worst. I do not wish for any harm to befall him."

Darcy, who had been staring at Elizabeth the entire time she spoke, seemed to awake from a daydream.

"My darling Elizabeth, I do not wish for him to come to harm either. As soon as you left for church, two of the stablehands followed him and confirmed he was safe at the Meryton Inn. While I spent very little time with him, I am confident he will be well."

Elizabeth sighed. "Thank you, darling. That is very comforting."

Darcy kissed her hand.

"I want you to be happy, Elizabeth."

"And I want you to be happy," Elizabeth said. "I know you have been through so much with your sister, and it would give me great pleasure to see you content. I rejoice at the thought of being your wife, and the mother of your children."

Darcy laughed and kissed her hand again.

"For a young lady who tended to run away from love, you are certainly not afraid of anything now."

"It was not that I disliked love," Elizabeth said. "I just never felt sure enough about it to act upon it."

Darcy nodded.

"I understand that. I felt the same way, until you."

"I am still not sure," she said and leaned her head on his shoulder. "It's probably too much to ask to find love, true love, in a world when so many people do not believe in it."

Darcy kissed the top of her head. "I believe in it with all my heart, Elizabeth. And this Christmas, I have found it."

Elizabeth looked up at him. "I love you, Fitzwilliam."

He smiled.

"And I love you, my darling Elizabeth."

Epilogue

ELIZABETH - ONE YEAR LATER

It had been one year since Elizabeth Bennet's life changed forever, and eleven months since she became Mrs. Elizabeth Darcy. Three months earlier, Helena legally became the daughter of Fitzwilliam and Elizabeth, and in November, Elizabeth gave birth to William George Darcy.

Christmas at Longbourn this year was sure to be one of glorious exultation and festivities.

More than just the Darcys celebrated, for young Kitty and her husband spent the holiday at Longbourn as well. Kitty was now sister-in-law to a countess, and though she wished she had been the first to marry, she was forced to admit that her sister was very happy. She only wished that she could have had a child like Elizabeth and Jane.

It was Christmas morning, a day the family was to spend at Longbourn. After a hearty breakfast, the men went to the library to drink port and the ladies retired to the parlor.

Elizabeth sat back, looked around and saw her family, her little girl, and her baby in her arms. She suddenly sighed with contentment. Jane laughed at her sister and smiled.

"I never thought I would see you so taken with domesticity, but I am overjoyed you have found it to be such a blessing."

Elizabeth smiled.

"I would not trade it for anything."

"Nor would I," Jane said and looked over at her sister. "I never could have imagined what it was like to be loved so dearly by someone."

"I assure you," Elizabeth said and looked over at Darcy in the other room. "I know."

"I am so happy for both of you," Jane said. "You both deserve every happiness you find."

"As do you."

Jane smiled and looked down. "I do not know what I did to deserve such good fortune."

"I do, though," Elizabeth said. "You are not just kind and caring, but you have been a friend to me during the happiest times and the most difficult. You knew when I needed you and you were there. I can never thank you enough for the felicity you have always brought to me."

Jane smiled and reached for her sister's hand. "I love you, Lizzy."

Darcy appeared in the parlor with a tray of tea and biscuits and set it down, then took little Will from Elizabeth's arms.

"Mrs. Hill was on her way with Christmas biscuits, but I wanted to deliver these delicious treats. And steal a few moments with my son. Mrs. Bennet, that was a delicious Christmas feast. You outdid yourself this year."

Mrs. Bennet smiled and puffed up with pride.

"Thank you, Fitzwilliam."

Darcy kissed his little son on the forehead and handed him back to his mother. He then turned to his wife and took her hand.

"And I did not want to miss my opportunity to wish you a very merry Christmas, my darling Elizabeth."

Elizabeth never felt so content.

"Thank you, Fitzwilliam. I wish you the same."

Darcy kissed her hand.

"Elizabeth, love, I am in need of your assistance."

"My assistance?"

Darcy nodded. "Yes. I want to give you a present this Christmas, but I need your help."

Elizabeth smiled. "Of course. Anything."

"I need you to open this for me." He took a box from his coat and handed it to her. Elizabeth opened the box, and inside was a silver watch with colorful rubies on the face of it. She had heard of watches made for ladies but had yet to see one herself.

"My goodness. It is beautiful."

"Only half as beautiful as you, my love," Darcy said as fastened the watch to her wrist.

With her husband and her children by her side, and her family all around, Elizabeth was overwhelmed with love. This truly was the best Christmas of her life...

Until next year.

~ *The End* ~

Elizabeth's Christmas Dream

One

"Mama! Where are aunt and uncle? They were meant to arrive hours ago!"

Elizabeth did not know why Lydia fretted so, as she had little interest in the Gardiners' visit to Longbourn for Christmas, though she quite suspected it had more to do with the possibility of a gift than the pleasure of seeing her family for the holiday. Still, Lizzy could not help but worry about her beloved aunt and uncle. They were meant to arrive at Longbourn for Christmas hours earlier and yet they still had not so much as received word from them. Mrs. Bennet had not ceased her pacing since tea.

"I do not know *where* they are, Lydia, or I would not be quite so worried, now would I? Mr. Bennet, perhaps we should prepare a party to search the roads for them? The snow has grown ever so furious!"

Mr. Bennet, who had remained in his chair by the fire, did not share his wife's growing concern. "Dearest, I am sure the snow has slowed their carriage and they have only been delayed. Worrying yourself into sickness will not increase the speed of their arrival."

The Bennet family had spent days preparing Longbourn for Christmas, covering every inch of the house with ivy and holly and rosemary gathered from surrounded woods. Candles had been lit and a yule log was waiting to be lit. The younger Bennet daughters could speak of nothing but the Christmas dinner, and while the older girls kept their manners, they too were eager to eat around the table with their family.

But there was no question that concern over Mr. and Mrs. Gardiner's delay had begun to dull the spirits in the Bennet household, even among those such as Kitty, who were usually concerned for little more than their own trifles. Jane, who had been engaged in her needlework as a distraction, was at last forced to engage as she too simmered over with nerves.

"Papa, perhaps mama is correct. Uncle and aunt are so delayed, and they rarely are anything other than early," Jane said.

Mr. Bennet lowered his brow as if he were considering his family's request, but their conversation was interrupted by a sudden knock on the door.

"At last!" Mrs. Bennet cried as she jumped from her chair and hurried to the door at pace no one in the household had ever seen her dash before. They followed her to the entrance, excited that their missing relatives had finally arrived. But when Mrs. Bennet opened the door, it was not the Gardiners standing on the other side.

Instead, it was Mr. Fitzwilliam Darcy. His cheeks were rosy from the cold and he appeared as if he had been walking for miles in the snow. Each of the Bennets appeared surprised at the sight of him, though each also had their very different reasons. Elizabeth had not seen Mr. Darcy since their disastrous dance at the Netherfield ball and she was quite aghast to see him now, especially when she expected her Aunt Gardiner, with whom she intended to discuss the whole dreadful affair.

"Mr. Darcy! You appear as if you are frozen to the bone.

Please, come inside and warm yourself by the fire," Mr. Bennet said.

But Darcy held up his hand to intercede. "I am most grateful for your offer, but I am afraid I am here on a matter of some urgency. I was riding to Netherfield from town when I came upon your relatives, the Gardiners, stranded in the snow. The axle had broken on their carriage and they were in quite some manner of distress. Their driver had gone for help hours before my arrival and had never returned. I made an attempt to repair their carriage, but it was beyond fixing."

Mrs. Bennet began to fuss before Mr. Darcy had even finished his story, and it was clear there was more to be told.

"Calm yourself, Mrs. Bennet. Let Mr. Darcy finish. Mrs. Hill," he called out, "please fetch Mr. Darcy a cup of hot cider."

Darcy nodded gratefully and continued. "I offered them my horse to ride to their destination and said I would walk but they refused. They said they were too cold to ride. In truth, I knew it was better that I ride ahead, and came straight here, hoping we might take your carriage to retrieve Mr. and Mrs. Gardiner. They are not far but we must leave with haste. The snow is only growing more impossible by the moment."

Mr. Bennet nodded and turned to his daughters and wife. "The gentleman is right. Mr. Darcy and I will take the carriage before the road from Longbourn is completely impassable. Then we will return with your uncle and aunt. Mr. Darcy, you will stay with us for the holidays. The snow looks to be getting worse and leaving our home might not be an option soon. It is the very least we can do for the kindness you have offered our family."

Darcy protested but Mrs. Bennet would hear none of it. "Of course, you will stay. Now please, begin your journey before you are all lost, and Christmas is quite ruined for the whole family."

"Mama!" Elizabeth cried, shocked at her mother's impropriety. But neither Mr. Darcy nor Mr. Bennet seemed concerned as her father gathered his coats and they hurried out into the severe weather.

After the gentlemen left, the Bennet ladies gathered around the fire and tried to enjoy the cider that Mrs. Hill brought them, but they were all consumed by many different worries. As everyone else vexed about Mr. Bennet and the Gardiners as they pressed through the snow, and while Elizabeth shared their concern, she also felt the terror of knowing that Darcy was going to spend Christmas at Longbourn. She could not even fathom looking across the table at the Christmas feast and seeing Mr. Darcy's face, especially after their last conversation. How could she even summon the courage to do so?

It was over an hour before the front door opened again, which sent all of the Bennet women running back into the entrance. A common sigh of relief filled the room at the sight of Mr. Bennet and the Gardiners, exhausted and cold, but alive and healthy. Mr. Darcy stood behind them courteously, as if he wished to give the family time to revel in their joys.

"Brother! Are you well? Did you not freeze out there in the snow?" Mrs. Bennet cried as she embraced Mr. and Mrs. Gardiner.

"It was cold, to be sure, sister, and were it not for our champion, we might very well have turned into snow ourselves out there in the woods. We are quite lucky to be safe in your lovely, warm home, but we cannot help but wonder what happened to our rider."

Mr. Darcy gave a gentle cough. "I *could* go out and search for him, if you so wish."

Mrs. Bennet scoffed. "Nonsense. I am quite sure he is at the pub right now, drinking and enjoying his own fire. I have never trusted that driver and I have told you so for years, brother."

The family dismissed Mrs. Bennet's ranting and chose instead to center on their happiness that they were at last all together once again. For a moment, Lizzy forgot that Mr. Darcy was even there, but then her father reminded her once again.

"Mr. Darcy, words cannot express our gratitude for your assistance in rescuing our family. Mrs. Hill will make up a spare room for you and you will stay here until the storm clears. We will be happy to have you for the holidays!"

Elizabeth swallowed down a nervous cry that threatened to escape and instead, nodded happily.

"Of course, the more, the merrier!" she said, her nerves showing. Mr. Darcy watched her, his eyes measuring Lizzy thoughtfully from head to foot, giving her a shiver.

As she would never miss an opportunity to impress a fine gentleman like Darcy, Mrs. Bennet immediately set about getting the house ready for her new visitor, as well setting a supper table that would make Darcy aware what a fine house Longbourn was. Mrs. Hill and the cooks began getting the table ready as the Gardiners briefly retired to their chambers to warm themselves and change for the meal. Mr. Bennet's valet accompanied Mr. Darcy to his guest room in order to aid him in changing into borrowed clothing, as the Bennet women hurried about in a fit of excitement over their visitor.

"I can hardly believe Mr. Darcy will be spending Christmas with us, mama! We must show him a wonderful time, so that when he returns to Netherfield, he can tell Mr. Bingley and his sisters that we were exceptional hosts," Kitty said with delight.

Mary shook her head. "Christmas is about the celebration of the birth of our Lord, Kitty. Not acting as if we are desperate to be adored by the richest men of Meryton and London. Remember yourself!"

Kitty and Lydia ignored their most proper sister and ran off into the kitchen to see if the supper was ready. Jane helped Mrs. Bennet set the extra seat at the table, leaving Elizabeth unsure of what to do with herself. As everyone else was busying themselves with the evening's preparations, Elizabeth made her way to the sewing room, where she had hidden the small gifts she had made for her family. She opened the cabinet to ensure they were still safe, as her younger sisters were well-known for their intruding, but everything seemed to be in its place.

Content, Elizabeth closed the cabinet and almost jumped out of her skin. Mr. Darcy was standing on the other side of the door...

And she had no idea how long he had been there.

Two

"**M**r. Darcy," Elizabeth gasped, her heart pounding in her chest. "You gave me a start."

Darcy gave a quiet smile.

"Oh, I am sorry. I did not mean to frighten you. I was merely looking for something to read that might entertain me later tonight in the room your parents have provided for me. You were the only one about and I wanted to inquire about your own reading material."

Elizabeth rolled her eyes as she set down the presents. She did not particularly wish to share any of her favorite books with this man who all but mocked her intelligence not so long ago.

"I am not very well read, I am afraid. They interfere with my needlepoint so."

Darcy appeared genuinely surprised.

"Is that so? I am quite fond of them myself. The excitement of the evening has left me quite restless, and I thought I might find something that would stir my mind. I do not think I will sleep tonight."

Elizabeth furrowed her brow and crossed her arms over her chest.

"You will have to ask my father. His study is the second room down the hall. I am sure he will be happy to help you choose something."

It quickly became clear that he did not intend to leave her alone. Mr. Darcy approached Elizabeth and touched one of the pairs of mittens she had knitted for Jane.

"I am sorry. I did not mean to offend you. I am not accustomed to being in the company of ladies who read frequently. I forgot you are not one of those women."

Elizabeth scoffed. "Well, I am not one of those women. I am not one of those women at all. But as you once considered me to be quite dull, I did not see the point in sharing my interests with you."

Darcy nodded sadly.

"I should apologize again. I was wrong in my evaluation of you, so I beg that you will forgive me."

Elizabeth was intrigued by his insistence that she was not as she seemed. He was trying very hard to convince her of this fact and she was not certain why.

"Is it so wrong to be an intelligent woman?"

Darcy smiled.

"I did not say you were not intelligent. On the contrary, I believe that you are quite intelligent and are also very lovely in the candlelight."

Elizabeth blinked, her heart beating rapidly in her chest.

"I am not sure how to respond to that."

"You have no need to respond. I know I have been harsh in my criticism of you, but I vow to behave like a proper gentleman this Christmas."

Elizabeth turned away from his intense gaze and went back to organizing the gifts, though they needed no further organization. When she looked back up at Mr. Darcy, he was practically studying her. She cleared her throat before she spoke.

"I appreciate your apology. I will accept your change of heart.

But I have been under the impression that at least in part, the reason you have held an opinion of me is the belief that my family is unworthy of your company."

Darcy looked surprised. "Is that what you believe?"

Elizabeth turned to him, her eyes wide.

"You said as much at the assembly in town."

Before Darcy could answer, the sound of Mrs. Bennet's voice from the end of the hallway startled them both.

"Elizabeth! Elizabeth, where are you? It is almost time for supper! Mrs. Hill needs your help with the serving! Elizabeth!"

"Coming, mama! I shall be there in one moment!" she called back, hoping that would be enough to pacify her mother. When she was sure her mother had moved on to other business, she turned back to Fitzwilliam. "Mr. Darcy, while I appreciate your apology, and your kind words, I think it would be better if..."

"Elizabeth!" Mrs. Bennet appeared in the doorway, her hand over her heart. "Oh, there you are. We have a situation in the dining room. I need your help to sort it out. Oh, it is awful!"

Elizabeth nodded in apology at Darcy and then hurried away to the dining room, her heels clacking on the hardwood floor. Mrs. Bennet held the door to the dining room open for Elizabeth as she sighed with impatience.

"Mama, I was in the middle of a conversation."

Mrs. Bennet acted as if she had not heard her daughter speak at all.

"Thank goodness you are here. We have a serious problem."

Elizabeth's eyes widened as she took in the sight of the dining room table. The room had been decorated with a profusion of holly and ivy, and ribbons had been tied to each of the chairs. The table was filled with food, and the place settings looked glorious. Elizabeth could not understand why her mother was fretting so.

"Everything looks wonderful, mama. I do not understand."

Mrs. Bennet pointed to the center of the table. "The goose, my dear girl. Your sister, Kitty, the silly girl, was meant to mind it while Mrs. Hill tended to other things. And I fear it burned!"

Elizabeth took a deep breath and held back a laugh. She was unable to keep from smiling, and her mother looked at her with frustration.

"Mama, it is only a goose."

Mrs. Bennet shook her head.

"No, my dear, it is not just a goose. It is truly an embarrassment. I am certain that Mr. Darcy will think that we are completely incapable of putting on a good supper. What if he tells all his society friends that we ruined his Christmas?"

She seemed genuinely distraught.

"Mama, I am certain he will not ridicule us over it."

"Oh, but he will! How could he not? He is a gentleman, and accustomed to the finest things. And we can not even provide him with a Christmas Eve goose?"

Elizabeth embraced her mother and gave her a kiss on the cheek.

"You go and distract our guests with a holiday game. I will find Mrs. Hill and we will fix the goose. Everything will be fine, mama. I promise."

She hurried her mother out of the dining room and took a deep breath. If it was up to her to save Christmas for her traumatized family, then save Christmas she would...

One way or another.

Three

As Mrs. Bennet gathered the bustling household in the drawing room to play a round of Rhymes, Elizabeth and Mrs. Hill attempted to salvage the goose in the kitchen. While Kitty had, indeed, allowed the skin of the goose to burn by neglecting to turn the bird on the spit, it was not as dire as their mother made it seem. A few scrapes with a large knife and a good basting with a berry sauce were all it took to make the goose look as delicious as it had earlier in the evening. It only took an hour for them to deliver a gorgeous goose to the dining room table.

Elizabeth surveyed the table with a smile.

"Mrs. Hill, I think we have saved the meal, and possibly Christmas itself."

The housekeeper clapped her hands together happily and adjusted some of the side dishes, which they had warmed over the fire so they would be hot for the goose.

"Everything looks wonderful, Miss Elizabeth. Would you like me to fetch the family and Mr. Darcy from the drawing room?"

She shook her head. "I will do it. Please, go and rest your feet. I will make you a plate once everyone is sitting."

"Oh, Miss Lizzy," she protested, "you do not need to…"

"It is Christmas Eve, Mrs. Hill, and you are family. Now go."

The housekeeper hurried out as Elizabeth left to find her family. She was surprised to find Darcy joyously playing Rhymes with the Bennets and Gardiners as if he had always been a part of their household.

"Everyone," she interrupted, "dinner is served. If you would kindly return to the table, we can eat."

Darcy looked up at her from his place on the floor, his eyes shining with mischief.

"Ah, Christmas Eve dinner! My favorite."

Elizabeth looked at him, unsure of whether he was making a joke or not.

"Yes," she began, "the goose is very nice."

"Not the goose," Darcy corrected her. "The company."

Elizabeth flushed and looked away, but not before she caught a glimpse of a smile in his eyes.

With a bit of careful maneuvering and a few words of protest from Lydia as she was pushed away from Mr. Darcy, everyone found their places at the table and the meal began. Mrs. Bennet looked more relaxed than she had for days. She even took time to compliment Elizabeth on the bird. The Gardiners looked upon their niece with pride, and she could not help but beam with delight.

When the first course was over, Darcy stood up and began to clear his throat. Everyone became quiet, and he looked at Elizabeth.

"As we are all gathered here together, I would like to make a toast. To Mr. and Mrs. Bennet, who have not only provided us with a fine meal but who have been the most wonderful hosts. The table more than feels the warmth of their presence. And to Mrs. Gardiner and Mr. Gardiner, who braved great danger to spend Christmas with their family. And to all the Bennets, who have provided a home for me this season. But especially to Miss Elizabeth Bennet, who has a fire in her heart that warms the whole room."

Mrs. Bennet looked as if she would burst into tears, and Elizabeth blushed to the tips of her toes.

"Well," she began, "Mr. Darcy, we are greatly indebted to you for rescuing our dear Aunt and Uncle Gardiner from the snow. Any toast should surely be in your honor."

Darcy bowed his head before sitting down again. As the meal continued, Elizabeth could not help but to think about the words he had spoken. They warmed her soul, but she did not know what to say to the gentleman. If he had not shown up at their door that night, she might never have thought about Fitzwilliam Darcy again. And yet here he was, saying such kind, thoughtful things about her. What had changed between them in such little time?

The goose was served with delicious bread, potatoes, and other vegetables. As soon as everyone was done eating, Elizabeth and Mrs. Hill began to remove the dishes from the table, and Darcy offered to help as well. They tried to discourage him but he would not be deterred.

"Miss Elizabeth," he whispered as they walked away. "May I ask you a question?"

"Yes, of course."

"Who prepared the goose? It was delicious."

Elizabeth laughed.

"It was a family effort. My mother always insists that we serve goose on Christmas Eve. She views it as a special treat, and she never wants to miss out on it."

Darcy nodded as he placed a stack of plates on the sideboard.

"I understand. I am quite fond of our family's Christmas traditions as well."

Elizabeth turned to look at the gentleman and was surprised to see he appeared sad. "I am sorry that you are not spending the holiday with your own family, or your friends. You have given up so much to save our Christmas. I do not know how we will ever thank you."

"Miss Bennet," he said softly, "you and your family have given me a wonderful Christmas. And, if you will excuse me for a moment, I would like to give you something as well."

Elizabeth blushed and nodded to him. He took a candle and made his way up the stairs to the room where he would be sleeping. He returned a minute later with a large book in his hand.

"I do not know whether you were familiar with the writings of Alexander Pope," he said as he took a seat next to Elizabeth. "But this is a collection of his poetry. I, personally, am very fond of his work."

"I read him frequently," she said. "He is one of my favorites."

"I am glad to hear it. I thought you might like to keep this as a gift. It was in my satchel and I have already read it many times. You will give it a good home, I am sure."

Elizabeth felt her eyes begin to water, and she could not think of a thing to say. In her mind, she chastised herself for her lack of grace. The gentleman had just given her a gift, a beautiful, thoughtful gift, and all she could say was thank you.

"Thank you, Mr. Darcy."

He smiled at her and tapped her arm with his finger.

"Please, call me, Fitzwilliam."

She blushed and looked down at the floor before smiling at him.

"Thank you, Fitzwilliam. I shall treasure this always."

When Mrs. Hill returned to the kitchen, Darcy quickly stood and bowed to both women.

"I think I will join the other gentleman in the drawing room for a brandy. Ladies."

The housekeeper hurried over to collect the dishes and looked at the book in Elizabeth's lap.

"Where did that come from, Miss Lizzy?"

She brushed her fingers across the cover of the lovely book.

"A gift, from Mr. Darcy."

Mrs. Hill tutted thoughtfully.

"He seems like a decent sort of fellow. Much nicer than everyone made him seem. Perhaps it is not so terrible that he came for Christmas after all."

Elizabeth smiled as she held the book to her chest.

"No, Mrs. Hill. Perhaps it is not."

Four

∞

After the dinner was cleared and the family was gathered in front of the fire, Mary sat at the piano and began to play carols. The entire time they sang, Elizabeth could not help but notice that Mr. Darcy was watching her carefully, with a thoughtful smile on his face. She found that she was unable to keep her own eyes off of him. Though she would not have thought it possible, she found his presence far more comforting than she had remembered. She watched as he gazed at her throughout the carol and blushed as she looked away.

Once the candles were lit, everyone settled down to enjoy the evening. They drank tea and brandy, played games, and spoke of the adventures of the day. The Gardiners were grateful to be able to sit by the fire and take comfort in the warmth that had been missing from their lives. The rest of the night was spent in happy conversation and laughter. Even Mary managed to put on a cheerful face for a change.

At some point, everyone began to make their way up to bed as the evening came to an end. It was not long before Elizabeth and Darcy were the only ones left in the drawing room. The candles were almost burned down, but the fire was still crackling pleasantly, and the snow falling outside was beautiful.

"Can I interest you in a last glass of port before we retire, Miss Bennet?" Darcy asked as he began pouring one glass.

"Yes, please."

He offered her a glass and they sat in silence, each of them gazing into the fire.

"Thank you again for the book," she said. "It was very kind of you."

Darcy smiled.

"I enjoyed your company very much, Miss Bennet. It would be my pleasure to give you a personal tour of my library at Pemberley some day."

Elizabeth felt butterflies take flight in her stomach. Did he truly just extend an invitation to his home? She swallowed nervously.

"I would enjoy that very much."

He nodded and turned to look at her.

"You are very beautiful tonight, Miss Bennet. I must say that you look particularly radiant in the firelight."

Elizabeth shook her head and smiled at him.

"I do not know about that, Mr. Darcy."

"And I would not claim such a thing unless I were absolutely sure of it."

Elizabeth took a sip of her wine and laughed. "You look quite handsome yourself this evening. Quite dashing actually."

He chuckled and raised his glass.

"Then a Merry Christmas to us both, the most beautiful people in this drawing room."

Elizabeth looked up at him, feeling as though this was a dream. He smiled at her.

"Miss Bennet, you must know that I have had feelings for you for quite some time, though I have never said a word. I am so glad that we finally have had this chance to spend time together, odd though the circumstances may be. I can think of no one else whom I would rather sit with by the fire."

Elizabeth's cheeks flushed as she blushed at his frankness. She looked away to hide her response. "Why now? When our first meeting was so terrible?"

He reached over and lifted her chin with his finger so that she was looking at him.

"Because you are the most beautiful, most unique woman I have ever met."

Elizabeth could feel her heart beating faster. He was looking at her in a way that made her feel as though he desired her very soul. It was a powerful feeling. Her heart was pounding as she searched his face. She found it difficult to breathe. As she looked at him, he returned her gaze with the same intensity. It was as though he was about to kiss her, and she was on the very edge of letting him.

"Mr. Darcy," she whispered as she leaned toward him.

Just as their lips were about to meet, Elizabeth heard the sound of footsteps in the hallway.

"I do not wish to interrupt you," Mrs. Hill said as she walked into the room. "But I wished to tell Mr. Darcy that his room is prepared if he wishes to retire."

Darcy and Elizabeth looked up at the housekeeper, who was visibly startled by their closeness.

"Mrs. Hill..." Elizabeth started. But shook her head.

"Do not mind me," Mrs. Hill said. "I can return at another time."

"No," Darcy answered quickly. "I am quite tired. In fact, Miss Bennet was about to direct me to my room. I was so sleepy, I thought I might faint dead away. Thank you for your assistance, Miss Bennet. May you have pleasant dreams."

He hurried from the room behind Mrs. Hill, who seemed content that she had misunderstood the situation. But Elizabeth could not help but wonder what might have happened had the housekeeper not appeared when she did...

And what the meant for her changing relationship with Mr. Darcy.

Five

Elizabeth woke the next morning to the sounds of the household gathered downstairs for Christmas. Because of the snow, they would not be able to make their way to church, which meant Mrs. Bennet and Mrs. Hill would go out of their way to make the morning special. She could smell the Christmas buns baking, coffee boiling on the stove, and the scent of pine mingled with both deliciously. Elizabeth dressed as quickly as she was able, then rushed down to join everyone for breakfast.

When she ran into the dining room, she found that her family was already sitting at the table, laughing and chatting. Mrs. Hill and Jane were bringing trays of bread, fruit, and jam to the table, so Elizabeth hurried to help them.

"Why did you not wake me?" Elizabeth asked Jane as she fetched the coffee and a tray from the sideboard. "I could have helped!"

Jane smiled and gave her sister a gentle nudge.

"I heard you were up quite late last evening. I thought you might wish to get a bit of rest, so I offered to assist Mrs. Hill with breakfast."

Elizabeth scowled at their housekeeper as she hurried past

them with butter and cream, careful not to make eye contact. Secrets did not remain secrets at Longbourn, so Elizabeth knew that word would spread that she and Darcy had been alone in the drawing room last night. She only hoped the gossip could wait until after Christmas.

"Have mama and papa heard?" Elizabeth whispered as she followed Jane out of the kitchen. Her sister shook her head.

"Not yet. I told Mrs. Hill to mind her tongue to the rest of the family. She could tell her stories tomorrow. You should not have to confront mama's questions on Christmas Day."

Elizabeth sighed with relief.

"Thank you, Jane. I was not anxious to discuss this over the Christmas buns."

In a way, it was a relief that the news had not yet spread beyond the housekeeper. For if Mrs. Bennet, Lydia, and Kitty were to find out about her evening in Mr. Darcy's company, she was sure they would be very excited. There would be time to discuss it later.

"And are you going to at the very least tell *me* what happened with Mr. Darcy last night?" Jane whispered as they carried the trays of food to the table.

"Not yet," Elizabeth laughed. "If we do not get this food to the table, I believe that Mrs. Hill might go mad."

Elizabeth hurried back into the kitchen to fill a few more trays with cups as Jane returned to the dining room.

"What were you and your sister whispering about in here?" Darcy asked as he suddenly appeared behind Elizabeth. He startled her so much, she almost dropped the tray in her hands. It was by sheer luck alone that he was able to catch the front and prevent it from falling.

"Mr. Darcy!" she cried, her cheeks reddening. "You frightened me!"

He smiled and handed her back the tray.

"My apologies, Miss Bennet. I did not mean to startle you. I was merely following you into the dining room, wishing to ask you a question."

Elizabeth took a deep breath as they walked toward the dining room.

"Yes, Mr. Darcy?"

Darcy paused a moment before he spoke.

"I was wondering if you would join me in the study after breakfast. I had a few questions about Longbourn and would like your help finding the answers."

Elizabeth was shocked he would ask to speak alone again after their last meeting. Yet, she was intrigued.

"Certainly, Mr. Darcy. I would be happy to help in any way I can," she answered quietly. But all she could think was: *he wants to speak to me. Alone.*

It was almost too much to comprehend.

The breakfast finished quickly, as everyone was anxious to exchange gifts and tell stories by the fire. Once their bellies were filled and the dishes were cleared, Darcy and Elizabeth snuck away to her father's study. It was a place that she always loved— a small, perfectly-proportioned room with two red velvet chairs that matched the chaise in the corner. The walls were covered with landscapes of the English countryside, as well as portraits of her family members from generations before. And there was always a new book to read on the desk that her papa did not mind her stealing away once he was done.

Elizabeth sat in one of the chairs and placed her hands in her lap nervously.

"What is it that you wished to know about Longbourn, Mr. Darcy?"

Darcy took a seat next to her. "I suppose I wish to know more about your situation with your cousin, William Collins? I overheard a conversation between your parents and the Gardiners. I do hope you do not find me presumptuous..."

Elizabeth did not wish to discuss the marriage that was

planned between her and her cousin in order for her family to remain at Longbourn. She told everyone they were not allowed to discuss the matter in front of her until the new year, and even then, she was not sure she wanted to talk about it ever again.

"It is not presumptuous but neither is it my favorite subject. If I do not marry William Collins, my family could be turned out with nothing should something happen to my father. I have requested that I not be reminded of the issue until January at the very least. It is hard to be merry when you dread the future."

Darcy leaned forward in his chair and rubbed his forehead with his hand.

"Forgive me, Elizabeth. I did not mean to bring up such an unpleasant subject. When I heard them speaking, I did not think it was about anything as horrible as this."

Elizabeth smiled at him and leaned forward as well. "You did not know. I appreciate your concern."

Darcy ran his fingers through his hair. "I still feel as if I have ruined your Christmas by bringing it up."

Elizabeth shook her head and shrugged.

"Mr. Darcy. There is no need for you to feel guilty. You did not know, and I am not angry. I am very glad you asked to speak with me."

She did not know if it was the cold or the thought of marrying William Collins, but a shiver spread throughout Elizabeth's body. Darcy did not even hesitate.

"You are freezing, Elizabeth. Here." He took off his jacket and placed it gently over her shoulders. "I feel as if I am wrapping a lovely Christmas present." Elizabeth smiled as Darcy sat back down. "You are too kind, Mr. Darcy."

"I am still very sorry that you are being forced into this," he said. "Nor will I judge you if you chose to marry Mr. Collins. Yet, I have to tell you that the idea of the two of you together is more than distasteful."

Elizabeth's cheeks flushed. "And if I felt the same way? If I preferred someone else to Mr. Collins?"

Darcy's face brightened.

"Do you?"

Elizabeth smiled and nodded. She had never been so happy in all her life, as it became clear where the conversation was headed.

"Yes, Mr. Darcy. I do."

Darcy stood from his seat and came to kneel in front of her.

"Then I think we have something to discuss with your mother and father."

Elizabeth's breath caught in her throat.

Yes, perhaps they did...

Darcy and Elizabeth returned to the drawing room to find the family prepared to exchange presents. Everyone had clearly grown impatient in their absence and was anxious to open their small packages. Elizabeth was glad she thought to fetch everything before they returned.

Lydia was, as always, the most restless.

"Lizzy! Where have you been? My lap is full of presents and mama would not let us open a single one until you returned. Where did you go?"

Elizabeth glanced at Darcy and then shook her head.

"Nowhere. Mr. Darcy simply wished to see father's recent acquisitions from the book store. Open your gifts, Lydia. Do not wait for me."

"Oh!" Lydia exclaimed excitedly. "I cannot wait."

"Merry Christmas," he whispered, and she quickly turned to him and smiled.

"And to you, Mr. Darcy. Merry Christmas."

"Lizzy! Are you not going to open your presents?" Kitty asked, her brow furrowed in irritation.

Elizabeth laughed as she lifted a stack of small packages wrapped in different colored paper from next to the fire.

"Of course I am, Lydia. I merely wished to see what everyone else received first. You know that is my favorite part."

One by one, Elizabeth opened each gift under the watchful eye of the gifter. Her parents gave her a new pen and Kitty a comb for her hair. From Lydia, she received a new knitting box and Jane gave her the most beautiful pair of lace gloves. Mary even handmade her a new purse. She was most surprised to receive a lovely silver ring from her Uncle and Aunt Gardiner that matched the ones given to her sisters. It was a truly thoughtful collection of gifts and more than she expected.

"You are all far too kind. Merry Christmas," Elizabeth said as she wiped a tear from her cheek. "This has truly been an unusual holiday, I think we can all agree on that. But our greatest gift has been the safe arrival of Aunt and Uncle Gardiner after their tumultuous trip."

The household nodded in agreement and Mrs. Bennet rushed over to hug her brother yet again. She had done so many times since they arrived at Longbourn. Mr. Bennet stood from his chair and placed his stack of new books on the ground, then lifted a bottle of wine from the side table.

"I think we should propose a toast before we begin to tell our Christmas ghost stories. I raise a glass to..."

Mr. Bennet's toast was interrupted by the sound of someone furiously knocking on the front door. They all looked out the window at the snow falling heavily, then at each other in surprise.

"Who could possibly be out there in this terrible weather?" Jane asked as she leapt from her seat and hurried to the door. Everyone followed her, rapt with curiosity. However, when Jane opened the door, it was as if all of the joy Elizabeth felt a moment before was swept out of her as if knocked from her by a gust of wind.

"Cousin William?" Mr. Bennet said in surprise. "What in the world are you doing here? In this terrible weather?"

Mr. and Mrs. Bennet rushed to bring Collins inside as Jane shut the door to the snow. The Gardiners led him to the fire and everyone scurried around to tend to his needs, but Elizabeth stood back in the doorway, afraid to get too close. William had not yet stated his purpose for coming to Longbourn on Christmas day, but whatever it was, she was not sure she wanted to hear it.

"I apologize for arriving without a proper invitation. I intended to come after the New Year but I am afraid I could not wait."

Mr. and Mrs. Bennet looked at each other, surprised.

"You are welcome, of course," Mr. Bennet said, "But what news was so important that you brave this snow on Christmas day?"

William took off his gloves and looked at Elizabeth, but only for a moment before addressing her father.

"I received correspondence from Lady Catherine de Bourgh only this morning with a most surprising request. She has asked that I accompany her on a trip to India in February. As we will be gone for some time, it is imperative that Elizabeth and I marry immediately in the new year. This way she can accompany us to India as Anne's companion."

Elizabeth did not remember which word caused her head to spin, but the last thing she saw before she fainted away was Darcy's face as he attempted to catch her as she fell...

Seven

When Elizabeth opened her eyes, every single person in Longbourn, except for William Collins, was standing over her and staring at her with worry. Elizabeth blinked several times, then sat up despite her aching head.

"Oh, that hurts. What happened?"

Jane and Darcy helped Elizabeth to her feet, then over to the sofa so she could lay down. Mary sat down next to her and patted her hand.

"You fainted, Lizzy. You fainted after Cousin William told us of his plan to accompany Lady Catherine to India after your wedding."

Elizabeth stared at Mary, then looked at the rest of her family standing around her.

"Surely he must have misunderstood. I can not be expected to go to India with..." She could not even finish the thought, it was so distasteful.

Mr. Bennet's brow furrowed.

"It *is* a very long way. Darling, if you do not wish to marry Collins, we can find an alternative. I do not want you to do this if you will be unhappy."

Elizabeth wanted to hug her father in joy but then she saw the expression on her mother's face. Mrs. Bennet stared at her in surprise, then covered her mouth with her handkerchief.

"Oh my! Oh my!" Mrs. Bennet said as she wiped her forehead with her handkerchief. "This will not do. Elizabeth, if you do not marry William, we will lose Longbourn! Mr. Bennet, tell her she must. She must!"

Mrs. Bennet turned to her husband who was already on his feet, his face grave and troubled. He shook his head at Mrs. Bennet and walked to the window, then turned to face them.

"I will not force my daughter to marry a man she does not love. It is not right."

Mrs. Bennet collapsed into a chair and buried her face in her hands as she began to sob.

"What have I done to deserve this? And on Christmas!" she cried.

Elizabeth stood up from the sofa and approached her father.

"Father, I am sorry. I have never meant to cause you distress."

Mr. Bennet sighed and patted Elizabeth's hand even as he looked at Mrs. Bennet sitting wailing in the chair. "We will find a solution, Lizzy. And it will be a solution that makes you happy."

"And I do not have to go to India? It is not that I do not *want* to go. Someday, I would like to. But not with William and that horrible..."

"That horrible who?"

William's voice startled everyone in the room and they all turned slowly in unison to see Collins standing in the hall. His face was pinched in a combination of frustration and confusion. Elizabeth did not know how to answer his question, but Darcy stepped in before she had the opportunity.

"Mr. Collins, it has been decided that Elizabeth will not be marrying you," Darcy said, surprising everyone. William scoffed and puffed out his chest.

"I beg your pardon?"

"I said," Darcy repeated, "that Elizabeth will not be marrying you. She will not be marrying you, nor anyone else, unless she chooses to. She is a woman of good standing, and she will marry for love or not at all."

Collins opened and closed his mouth several times like one of the fish in the pond.

"How dare you, sir. It is not custom to stick one's nose in someone else's marriage plans."

Elizabeth watched, her eyes wide, as Darcy took another confident step forward.

"Nor is it our custom to force a lady to marry a terrible little man she does not love."

Elizabeth and her father both gasped at Darcy's audacity.

"I am a man of God," Collins said, aghast. "Are you inebriated, sir?"

"No sir, I am most certainly not."

Elizabeth could not take her eyes off of Darcy. He had truly taken up for her in a way she did not expect, and never could have imagined after that night at the assembly. It was awe-inspiring.

"Then you are a fool, sir, and I will not listen to such nonsense," Collins said. But Elizabeth could hear no more of this arguing.

"William," Elizabeth said as she turned to him, "I am to be my own woman in this. I will make my own happiness, and I am not bound to marry any man. I will not marry you and I will not go to India. That is my final word on the matter."

Collins furrowed his brow.

"Then I suppose you will have to find another home for your family! Merry Christmas, indeed."

Then William took his coat and hat from the rack and stomped out into the snow, leaving everyone in the room stunned into silence. Mrs. Bennet finally lifted her head from her handkerchief.

"Well, now what are we going to do?"

Eight

"Should we have allowed him to leave?" Jane asked as she looked out the window at the snow. "It still looks quite ominous out there."

Mr. Bennet waved his hand dismissively. "He is stubborn. He will make it to the inn in due course and spread word of the indignities that have been committed against him before his boots have dried."

Uncle Gardiner and Darcy both laughed, but Elizabeth was not in a laughing mood. While she might be spared the indignity of becoming William Collins's wife, there was still the question of what would happen to Longbourn, to her family, if something were to happen to her father. She felt as if she failed her father, even if he was the one who encouraged her to end the engagement.

"Papa, I am glad you find this all so amusing, but mama is not wrong to be worried. What will we do? How will we secure the family's future if Longbourn can be taken away?"

Mr. Bennet sighed and looked at the ceiling, then stroked his chin and looked at his wife, who looked back at him with an eager expression.

"There is only one way to ensure the security and protection of Longbourn," Mr. Bennet said as he held out his hand to his wife. "Lizzy must find a match that suits *her*. Then we can worry about what comes next."

Mrs. Bennet gasped, then clapped her hands together and looked at Elizabeth with joyful eyes.

"Oh my! Oh my!" Mrs. Bennet said. "Of course! Lizzy, you will be married, and you will be happy, and we will not have to worry about losing Longbourn."

"Oh, there is no need to worry about that," Darcy said, surprising Elizabeth. He had been so quiet until that moment, Elizabeth almost forgot he was there. Everyone in the room turned to look at him. Mr. Bennet tilted his head in confusion.

"What is it you mean, Mr. Darcy?"

"I mean, I will be taking up the responsibility of caring for the residents of Longbourn," Darcy said.

Elizabeth felt the blood drain from her face. She looked to her father, who looked back at her with wide eyes.

"I beg your pardon?" Mr. Bennet said.

"I will not stand by and see Longbourn and its inhabitants suffer," Darcy answered. "I am sure we can come to an agreement that will allow the Bennet family to live in the style to which they have become accustomed."

Elizabeth walked over to him as casually as she was able, though she felt like she had bees in her feet. When she reached him, she whispered so only Darcy could hear her.

"Are you sure you wish to do this now? On Christmas?"

He took her hand and squeezed it gently. "I can think of no better time. Mr. and Mrs. Bennet, I would like to ask for the honor of your daughter Elizabeth's hand in marriage."

Her parents looked at one another in surprise, before turning back to Elizabeth and Darcy.

"Marriage? After one day?" Mr. Bennet asked with his eyebrow raised. "No," Darcy replied with a smile. "I have loved

Elizabeth since the very first time she shouted at me. I really have."

"Oh, what wonderful news!" Mrs. Bennet said, her eyes wide with joy.

Darcy turned and looked at Elizabeth.

"Do you think you could love me a little more by this time next week? That should be enough to justify a marriage, I think."

She smiled at him and took his hand in hers.

"I think that is a very doable proposition, Mr. Darcy."

Darcy smiled.

"Then I suppose we are engaged."

He squeezed her hand, and leaned over to kiss her on the cheek. Mrs. Bennet clapped her hands in delight and Mr. Bennet bowed to them both.

"It is a pleasure to see you together," Mr. Bennet said. "As if we needed a reason to toast again, let us all have a glass of wine and drink to this happy occasion."

Elizabeth's heart swelled as glasses were filled and embraces exchanged. Everything that had seemed so dire not so long ago felt joyous and full of promise now. And for that, she could thank the wonderful gentleman standing beside her.

ELIZABETH WAS TOO FILLED with excitement to sleep that night. She lay in her bed, thinking of all the good things that had happened that happened that Christmas. Her dearest aunt and uncle, rescued from the storm. The end of her engagement to William Collins and the beginning of one to Fitzwilliam Darcy. And finally, Fitzwilliam's promise to look after her family, no matter what happened with Longbourn. All of it was so wonderful, it seemed almost too good to be true.

This Christmas was like the most wonderful dream. And if she was dreaming, she never wanted to wake up...

~The End~

A Governess for Christmas

One

I could not help but feel a sense of desolation as I gazed upon the snow-covered gardens of Longbourn. The frosty December air settled heavily upon Meryton, and with it, the melancholy realization that three of my dear sisters had been swept away into the throes of matrimony, leaving behind only Kitty and myself to endure the coming festivities.

Christmas was fast approaching, and while our home was always filled with joy and laughter during the season, I found that my heart yearned for the presence of my beloved sisters, especially Jane. My days were now spent in the company of my dear parents and Kitty, who had grown more agreeable since Lydia's departure. Yet, I could not escape the gnawing dissatisfaction that plagued me with every passing day.

"Elizabeth!" called my mother from within the house, her voice shrill enough to pierce through the cold air. "A letter has arrived for you!"

Curiosity piqued, I hastened from the kitchen doorway, smoothing out my skirts as I made my way to the parlor where my mother eagerly waved the missive in the air.

"Here, my dear," she exclaimed, thrusting it into my hands. "It is from your Aunt Gardiner!"

Shivering from the sudden warmth of the fire, I carefully broke the wax seal and unfolded the parchment. As I skimmed the neat lines of my aunt's penmanship, I could not help but feel a stirring of anticipation. She wrote of a most intriguing opportunity - a position as governess in Lambton, a respectable village where they often stayed on holiday. The family sought someone to fill the post immediately, and my aunt believed that I was well-suited for such an occupation.

"Read it aloud, Elizabeth," urged my father, who had been observing the proceedings from his armchair by the fire.

With a nod, I cleared my throat and recited the contents of the letter, my voice growing more animated as I conveyed the urgency of the situation. The prospect of leaving Longbourn and embarking upon a new chapter in life was both thrilling and daunting. But with Jane's laughter now absent from the halls and the unspoken understanding that Kitty may soon follow our sisters into marriage, I could not deny the appeal this opportunity presented.

"Imagine, a governess!" exclaimed Kitty, her eyes wide with disbelief. "Would you truly consider it, Lizzy?"

I glanced at my sister, then at my parents, whose expressions were inscrutable, and felt a quiet resolve settle within me.

"Yes," I replied, my voice steady and determined. "I believe I shall."

"Elizabeth, my dear," my mother began, her eyes filled with worry and a hint of indignation, "you cannot seriously mean to leave us here at Longbourn, especially not at Christmastime!"

"Pray do not be alarmed, Mama. However, I believe it would be best for all of us if I were to accept this position. At least for a time, to see if it is a life to which I am well suited."

My father, who had been quietly observing our discussion, cleared his throat and spoke up in my defense.

"It may very well be a good opportunity for Lizzy, my dear. She has never shied away from hard work or responsibility, and this position might afford her a chance to make her own way in the world."

"Mr. Bennet, how can you say such things?" My mother's voice cracked with emotion as she addressed him, her hands wringing together in her lap. "Our daughter, a governess? And so far away! What will people think?"

"Let them think what they will," I interjected. "Mama, I must do something with my life, and I cannot bear the thought of spending Christmas mourning the absence of Jane and my other sisters. It is time for me to forge my own path, and this opportunity seems like a fitting place to begin."

Kitty chimed in, her expression troubled as she looked between me and our parents.

"I understand your need for change, Lizzy, but I do not wish to be left alone here at Longbourn either."

"Kitty, my love, you shall not be alone," I assured her, taking her hand in mine. "You have our parents, and I have no doubt that you too shall find your own happiness one day. You must know that I would never abandon you, but I must do what is best for my own heart and future."

"Besides," my father added with a wry smile, "I am certain that our dear Kitty will not lack for suitors once the news of her sister's departure reaches the ears of Meryton's eligible gentlemen."

"Mr. Bennet!" my mother exclaimed, scandalized by his jest, while Kitty simply blushed and looked away.

"Very well, Elizabeth," my mother conceded at last, wiping away a tear with the corner of her handkerchief. "If you are determined to go, then I suppose there is little we can do to stop you. But, promise me that you shall write often and return home as soon as you are able."

"Of course, Mama," I replied, embracing her tightly. "I shall miss you all terribly, but I know this is the right decision for me."

As I prepared for my imminent departure from Longbourn, I felt both excitement and trepidation coursing through my veins. This would be my first Christmas away from home, away from my family, but I was prepared for the adventure. I could not wait to see what this holiday in Lambton had in store for me.

Two

As I rode side by side in the carriage with my dear Uncle Gardiner, anticipation churned in my stomach. He had been kind enough to take me along on his visit to Derbyshire so that I might meet my potential employer, the gentleman who required a governess for his young wards. Despite the prospect for adventure, I found myself suddenly apprehensive. What kind of family might they be? Would they welcome her into their fold or treat her like staff?

Uncle Gardiner must have sensed my concern because he reached over and patted my hand comfortingly.

"Oh, Elizabeth, there is no need for such nerves. You are an intelligent and capable young woman. I have no doubt that you will be an asset to any household."

"Thank you, Uncle," I replied, grateful for his attempt to quell my anxiety, though it did little to help.

Just as I began to regain my composure, our carriage turned a corner, and I found myself staring in shock at the grand estate before us.

"Uncle Gardiner, is this Pemberley? But - but Pemberley is the home of Mr. Fitzwilliam Darcy!"

"That it is," my uncle confirmed, his eyes twinkling with amusement. "I thought it best not to mention his name before-hand, knowing your history with the gentleman. However, he has expressed a sincere interest in employing you. Do give him a chance, my dear. People can change, after all."

I could only manage a faint nod, remembering our unpleasant encounter at a ball in Meryton. It seemed impossible that I was now to be employed by the very man I had once despised. I struggled to wrap my mind around the thought as we continued up the long driveway.

Upon our arrival, there stood Mr. Darcy, waiting to greet us. His tall figure and dark, brooding countenance were just as I recalled. As our eyes met, I detected a glimmer of recognition in his gaze. To my great surprise, he greeted me warmly, as if we were old friends.

"Miss Bennet, welcome to Pemberley," he said, extending his hand to help me down from the carriage. "And Mr. Gardiner, it is a pleasure to see you again."

"Thank you, Mr. Darcy," my uncle replied, clasping Darcy's hand in a firm handshake.

"Please, come inside. I will show you the estate before we adjourn to the parlor for tea and biscuits," Mr. Darcy offered, leading us through the grand entrance of Pemberley.

As we toured the magnificent rooms, filled with elegant furnishings and exquisite works of art, my initial trepidation began to fade. Mr. Darcy was every bit the gracious host, describing the history of each room as he guided us along. I found myself curious about his motivations for this change in demeanor and wondered if perhaps my uncle's words held truth: people can indeed change.

Finally, we arrived at the cozy parlor, where a crackling fire warmed the room. A beautifully set table awaited us, laden with fragrant tea and an assortment of freshly made biscuits. It seemed that our host had spared no effort in making us feel welcome.

"Mr. Darcy," I began hesitantly, my fingers toying with the

edge of my teacup, "I must admit, I have concerns about accepting an offer of employment given our last encounter. I feel I must ask, do you even find me qualified to be your governess?"

The gentleman sighed and set down his teacup. "Please, allow me to apologize for my behavior that night at the assembly. There are no excuses, but I do hope you will consider this a new beginning before rejecting my offer."

I nodded as I considered his words, but could not help but notice my uncle, smiling and gesturing for me to accept. I began to wonder if I would even be allowed in the carriage should I change my mind. It was convenient, then, that I decided I would not do so.

"I will accept your offer of employment, Mr. Darcy."

"Then, Miss Bennet, it would be my utmost pleasure to introduce you to Joseph and Nicholas," Mr. Darcy replied, his expression softening into a genuine smile. "I will go call for them now."

"Thank you, Mr. Darcy," I said, feeling a mixture of trepidation and excitement at the prospect of embarking on this new chapter in my life.

Joseph and Nicholas walked politely into the room shortly thereafter, the two boys a picture in exact opposites. Joseph, the older, had hair almost as white as the winter snow and his eyes were a striking shade of emerald green. Nicholas, the little one, had raven black hair and eyes to match. They were both lively, energetic boys, who greeted me with an affection and kindness I had not expected. Their excitement at the arrival of their new governess was contagious, and I found myself looking forward to the challenge of guiding their education.

After the boys had been allowed to show me to their bed chambers, their nursery, and their own small library, Mr. Darcy finally intervened.

"Miss Bennet, if you would allow me, I shall ask Mrs. Reynolds to show you to your new room," Mr. Darcy offered with a smile. "I suspect you would like some time to acquaint yourself with your new home."

"Of course, thank you."

"Mrs. Reynolds," he called as the housekeeper appeared promptly at his summons, "please show Miss Bennet to her new quarters."

"Very well, sir," she said with a curtsy before turning to me. "Miss Bennet, if you would follow me, please."

As we ascended the grand staircase, I marveled at the opulence of Pemberley. The sheer size of my new room was astonishing – it was larger than the whole parlor at Longbourn. The furnishings were elegant yet comfortable, and the large windows afforded a stunning view of the snow-dusted gardens.

"Will this be satisfactory, Miss Bennet?" Mrs. Reynolds inquired, her eyes twinkling with anticipation.

"Oh, Mrs. Reynolds, it is far more than I could have ever imagined," I replied, unable to keep the awe from my voice.

"Then I shall leave you to settle in. If you require anything, please do not hesitate to ask."

As I unpacked my modest belongings and arranged them within the room, I could not help but feel unexpectedly at home. Despite our rocky history, Mr. Darcy had shown himself to be a generous employer, and I was eager to prove myself worthy of his trust.

I took a deep breath and sighed contentedly as I hung a string of holly garland that mama had put in my trunk, a bit of holiday spirit from home. In the quiet reflection of that moment, I allowed myself to entertain the possibility that perhaps, in time, Mr. Darcy and I might find a bit of understanding. One could always hope for miracles during the Christmas season.

Three

I had been at Pemberley for seven days when Joseph and Nicholas, though lovely children, began to tire me with their endless supply of energy. We were meant to work at their French lessons, which would be our third attempt to do so this week. Yet, the boys seemed far more interested in chasing each other around the nursery than in conjugating verbs. With a sigh, I tried once more to coax them back to their studies.

"Come now, *s'il vous plaît*," I pleaded, attempting to make my voice sound playful, despite the fact I felt decidedly less so.

Just as I was about to give up hope, the door swung open and Mr. Darcy entered the room. His expression was stern, his brows furrowed over dark eyes that seemed to see straight through to one's core. The moment the boys caught sight of him, they ceased their wild antics and scurried to their desks, sitting rigidly at attention.

"*Continuez, s'il vous plaît*," he said, gesturing at the children to go back to their reading. I nodded gratefully, though part of me wished he would stay and spend time with his wards. Since my arrival at Pemberley, I had seen little of him outside the formal dinners we shared with the rest of the household.

Once the boys were thoroughly absorbed in their work, Darcy turned to me.

"Miss Bennet, Christmas is fast approaching, and I was wondering if there is anyone you would like to invite to join us for the celebrations."

Startled by the question, I hesitated for a moment before answering.

"Well, sir, my uncle is traveling on business, but perhaps my Aunt Gardiner could come and stay? She has always been a great support to me, and I know she would enjoy experiencing Christmas at such a grand estate."

"Of course," he replied without hesitation. "I shall extend an invitation to her at once."

I felt an unexpected rush of affection for the gentleman, touched by his thoughtful offer. "Thank you, Mr. Darcy," I said with genuine gratitude. "Your kindness is most appreciated."

"Think nothing of it, Miss Bennet. It is the least I can do given your arrival at Christmas. I know Nicholas and Joseph will appreciate a nice full household, as well."

I glanced over at the boys, their heads bent studiously over their books, and felt a sudden urge to express what had been bothering me for days.

"Mr. Darcy," I began hesitantly, unsure of how he would take my suggestion, "might it be possible for you to spend some time with the children tomorrow? They have not seen much of you outside of meals this past week, and I believe they would benefit from your guidance and influence."

Darcy paused, his eyes meeting mine, and I could see him turning over the idea in his mind. After a moment, he nodded thoughtfully, then turned his attention to the boys, hands resting on his hips.

"What do you say, gentlemen?" he asked them, his tone suddenly warm. "Have I neglected you this week?"

The boys immediately jumped up from their desks, abandoning their books without a second thought as they raced to Mr. Darcy's side. To my surprise, they threw their arms around him in an affectionate embrace, and even more surprising was Darcy's response; he returned their hugs with equal warmth, a soft smile gracing his face.

"We know how hard you work, Mr. Darcy," Nicholas said as he looked up at his guardian with admiring eyes.

"But we have missed you," chimed Joseph, his cherubic face earnest and hopeful.

"I see," Darcy said, gently extricating himself from their enthusiastic embraces. The boys returned to their desks happily, their earlier mischief seemingly forgotten.

"Miss Bennet," Darcy addressed me, "while I do not believe the boys feel abandoned, you are correct. We should always take time for family, especially during the holidays. Tomorrow, we will all go for an invigorating walk in the gardens."

"In the snow?" I questioned, surprised by his proposal. The weather had been quite cold recently, and the ground was covered in a blanket of white.

"Of course in the snow, Miss Bennet," Darcy replied, heading towards the door. "I will make sure Mrs. Reynolds brings you a sturdy pair of boots just for the occasion."

With that, he left the nursery, and I found myself marveling at this unexpected new side of Mr. Darcy I had just witnessed. The tender affection he displayed with the boys was a far cry from the stern, unapproachable man I had first met. As I watched the boys practicing their French, I began to suspect that there was much more to this family than I initially thought...

And tomorrow would be an excellent way to discover more about them.

Four

As Darcy, the children, and I prepared ourselves for our snowy hike around Pemberley, Mrs. Reynolds appeared in the doorway of the parlor with an air of hesitance.

"Mr. Darcy, sir, we have an unexpected visitor... and they have brought luggage."

Darcy raised his eyebrow as he set his coat down on the chair. "A visitor? Today? Whoever could it be?"

"Miss Caroline Bingley," she said, her lips pursed in frustration. And as if summoned by the utterance of her name, the lady herself came barging in, her cheeks flushed from the cold.

"Fitzwilliam! What a pleasure to see you! I seem to have arrived ahead of my dear brother Charles, but I do hope I will not be a bother. Oh... the children. I forgot they would be here."

Surprise washed over me as I glanced at Darcy. I had not realized he had invited others to join us during our holiday celebrations. He stared back at Caroline, his irritation evident in the furrow of his brow.

"Miss Bingley, I only extended an invitation for Christmas to your brother. I did not expect to see you, as he specifically mentioned that you did not intend to be with him this year."

"But here I am, just the same," she proclaimed, a smirk gracing her lips.

Darcy sighed heavily, and it was clear to me that he was not thrilled with Caroline's unexpected arrival. He delayed our hike momentarily, gesturing for the boys to go to the nursery while he dealt with the situation. As I moved to follow them, Darcy reached out, asking me to stay.

"Miss Bennet—"

"Hurry, Miss Lizzy! I can not reach the book I wish to read," Joseph exclaimed, tugging at my hand and pulling me away despite Darcy's protests. While I followed the little boy, my curiosity was nonetheless piqued.

"Joseph, why did your cousin wish for me to stay behind with him and Miss Bingley?" I inquired, hoping the boy might shed some light on the matter.

"I really do not know, Miss" he mumbled, obviously annoyed. "But Miss Bingley is always bothering Cousin Fitzwilliam when she is here. It seems as if she is trying to marry him, so we have decided that we do not like her."

The disdain in his voice made me chuckle, but I could not help but consider that Miss Bingley might not be someone I could trust.

Time slipped away as I watched the children at play, their laughter and energy filling the nursery with warmth. The sound of footsteps approaching caught my attention, and I turned to see Darcy entering the room. His eyes met mine, a hint of amusement dancing within them.

"Are we ready for our snowy adventure?" he inquired, his voice carrying a note of excitement.

"Will Miss Bingley be joining us?" young Nicholas asked, his expression filled with trepidation.

"Miss Bingley will not be accompanying us," Darcy replied, the corners of his mouth twitching upward ever so slightly.

The children erupted into cheers, their enthusiasm uncontained. I could not help but mirror their joy, albeit more subtly. However, remembering my role as an adult, I gently chided them.

"Children, we must always be mindful of our manners, even when discussing those who are absent."

"Of course, Miss Lizzy," Joseph agreed, though the twinkle in his eye betrayed his true feelings.

Unable to resist myself, I turned to Darcy. "Why is it that Miss Bingley shall not be joining us?"

"Ah, well, you see, Caroline Bingley does not engage in activities that require physical or mental exertion of any kind," he answered, his tone playful yet laced with truth.

The image of Miss Bingley lounging idly while we enjoyed the crisp winter air brought a smile to my face. She certainly did not seem the type to fancy a walk in the snow but at least now the children could enjoy their afternoon.

"Everyone, please bundle up," Darcy announced, gesturing toward the assortment of coats, hats, and mittens laid out upon the chaise. "It is time to venture forth into the snow."

"Adventure awaits!" said Nicholas, eagerly donning his coat and hat.

As we all prepared for our outdoor excursion, I could scarcely contain my delight. The prospect of spending a carefree day in the snow with Mr. Darcy and the children warmed me from within. I surprised even myself at my sudden love of the winter cold, but it seemed my time at Pemberley was already changing my outlook on things for the better.

"Are you ready to go, Miss Lizzy?" Joseph asked, his voice muffled by the scarf wrapped around his face.

"Indeed, I am," I replied, beaming at the child. With anticipation in our hearts, we followed Darcy into the winter wonderland that awaited us outside the walls of Pemberley, leaving the specter of Miss Bingley far behind.

Five

As we walked into Pemberley's grand entrance, all bundled up to face the winter chill, the excitement of the young boys was palpable. Their cheeks were already flushed with glee at the prospect of exploring the grounds.

"Miss Bennet," said Darcy, offering his arm to me with a gallant bow, "are you ready for our little excursion?"

"That I am, Mr. Darcy," I replied, taking his arm and feeling my own cheeks grow warm, from the proximity to him. "I have been looking forward to seeing the beauty of Pemberley in winter."

"Then let us not delay any further," he declared, giving a nod to the footman who stood by the door. The great doors swung open, revealing a breathtaking scene of untouched snow blanketing the landscape.

"Look, Miss Lizzy!" cried young Nicholas, pointing towards the snow-covered gardens. "It looks like a world made entirely of the flour in cook's kitchen!"

"Indeed, it does seem that way, Nicholas," I replied, unable to suppress a smile at his enthusiasm.

"Come, come," urged Joseph, tugging on his brother's sleeve, "let us explore and find the perfect spot for a snowball fight."

"Very well," agreed Darcy, "but do remember to be careful and not wander too far."

"Of course, Cousin Fitzwilliam," chorused the boys, already bounding off into the snowy expanse with youthful energy.

As we stepped out into the crisp winter air, I could not help but shiver slightly, despite my thick pelisse and bonnet. However, the cold could not dampen my spirits, nor the warm feeling that blossomed within me whenever I was in the gentleman's presence.

The sunlight sparkled off the frozen branches of the trees, transforming them into a crystalline wonderland that took my breath away.

"My goodness, Mr. Darcy," I whispered in awe, "it is as though we have stepped into an enchanted world."

"It does, indeed, Miss Bennet," he agreed, his eyes reflecting the same admiration I felt for the snow-covered scene before us. "Pemberley often looks its finest during the winter months."

As we continued to walk, I noticed that the frozen pond nearby sparkled like a thousand tiny diamonds, capturing the sun's rays and sending them dancing across the surface. The sight was mesmerizing, and I found it difficult to tear my gaze away.

"Allow me to show you the path that winds around the pond," Darcy suggested, guiding me gently by the elbow. "There are some lovely views to be had from there."

"Thank you, Mr. Darcy."

We walked through the snowy landscape, leaving a trail of footprints behind us as Joseph and Nicholas raced ahead, their laughter ringing through the air. The gentleman led us along a winding path that skirted the edge of the frozen pond, pointing out various landmarks and sharing stories about the history of Pemberley.

"Over there," he indicated with a sweep of his arm, "is where my great-grandfather planted a grove of oak trees to commemorate the birth of his first son."

"Such a fitting tribute," I mused, admiring the stately oaks as they stood sentinel over the landscape. "And what of that small gazebo nestled amongst the trees?"

"Ah, that," Darcy said with a smile, "has a rather amusing story attached to it. My grandfather, who was known for being a bit of a romantic, built the gazebo as a tribute to his intended bride. Whenever guests went out to enjoy the gardens, he would declare his wife Queen of Pemberley and the gazebo her throne."

"Your family history is fascinating," I told him with a smile as I imagined visitors gathered around the gazebo, admiring the future Mrs. Darcy those many years ago.

"Thank you, Miss Bennet," he said warmly. "It brings me great joy to share these stories with someone who appreciates them."

As we continued our walk, I felt a growing sense of wonder at the beauty of Pemberley in winter, and an even greater sense of gratitude for the opportunity to experience it with Mr. Darcy by my side.

As we wandered further along the snowy path, the sun shining over the pristine landscape, I felt a sudden curiosity about Mr. Darcy's life beyond his role as master of Pemberley. Turning to face him, I asked, "Mr. Darcy, if I may be so bold, how did you come to be the guardian of Joseph and Nicholas? It is evident that you care for them deeply."

Darcy paused in his stride, surprise coloring his features.

"I must say, it has been some time since anyone asked me about the origin of the children. I have not shared the story with anyone outside the family since it happened." He took a moment to gather his thoughts before continuing. "My cousin, Colonel Fitzwilliam, and his wife tragically passed away from illness. As their closest relative, it fell upon me to assume responsibility for their sons, Joseph and Nicholas."

"Such a heavy burden to bear," I said sympathetically, my heart aching for the loss the children had experienced.

"Nothing compared to that of the children," he agreed, his voice laced with sorrow. "However, I have always believed that family is of the utmost importance, and I could not imagine abandoning my young cousins in their time of need. It is my duty to provide for them, just as I would my own sons."

I watched as Mr. Darcy gazed out at the wintry scene before us, the weight of his words hanging in the air. His dedication to his family was truly commendable.

"Your devotion to your family is admirable, Mr. Darcy," I said softly, unable to hide the warmth in my tone. "And I am certain that your cousins are grateful for your guidance and protection."

"Thank you, Miss Bennet," he replied, his eyes meeting mine. "Your kind words mean a great deal to me."

We continued our walk in companionable silence, the laughter of Joseph and Nicholas carrying through the crisp winter air as they chased one another across the snow-covered grounds. As I observed their joyous antics, I could not help but ponder the depth of Mr. Darcy's character – a man who, despite his wealth and status, not only embraced his responsibilities with grace but also cherished the bonds of family above all else. It was in that moment that I realized just how much my feelings for him had grown, and I knew that I could no longer deny the stirring of affection that blossomed within my heart.

Six

The air in the drawing room at Pemberley felt heavy with the weight of tension that hung between Caroline Bingley and myself. We sat across from one another, attempting to engage in polite conversation, yet every syllable seemed to be coated in a thin layer of ice. I glanced toward the window, knowing that Mr. Darcy and the boys were still in the stables, and silently prayed for their speedy return.

"Miss Bennet," Caroline began, her voice dripping with condescension, "I must say it is quite remarkable to see you here at Pemberley in such an esteemed capacity. Not many can boast of being worthy of the position of governess to Mr. Darcy's wards."

"Yes, Miss Bingley," I replied, trying my best to maintain composure. "It is an honor to be entrusted with the education and well-being of such delightful young gentlemen."

"Delightful as they may be, I cannot help but wonder if they might not have been better served by someone more...qualified. After all, your own social standing leaves much to be desired, does it not?"

My cheeks flushed with embarrassment, and I struggled to come up with a suitable retort. It was true; my family's modest background paled in comparison to the prestige of the Darcy name. However, I knew that Mr. Darcy had chosen me based on merit, not social status – a fact that only seemed to fuel Caroline's jealousy further.

"That may be true," I conceded, "but I believe Mr. Darcy values the quality of one's character above the size of one's estate."

"Oh, yes, character," she sneered, crossing her legs and adjusting her silk gown. "How fortunate for you that Mr. Darcy sees something in your character that others do not. Then again, perhaps he simply enjoys the company of those who share his penchant for brooding and solitude."

"Miss Bingley," I said, my voice trembling with suppressed anger, "it is not my place to question Mr. Darcy's preferences or motives. My sole concern is the well-being of his cousins, and I intend to carry out my duties to the best of my abilities."

"I would never suggest otherwise," she replied, feigning innocence as she sipped her tea. "I merely meant to remark upon the unique situation in which we find ourselves – you, a humble governess in the grand halls of Pemberley, and I, the sister of Mr. Darcy's oldest friend, relegated to observing from the sidelines."

"Surely you are aware," I countered, unable to hide my annoyance any longer, "that one's worth is not determined by their social standing alone."

"Such things, Miss Bennet, are only said by those with no social standing of which to speak."

The woman's eyes gleamed with a malicious delight as she continued her thinly veiled attack on my character.

"You know, Miss Bennet," she continued, her voice dripping with feigned sweetness, "I have heard some rather intriguing rumors about your past."

"Rumors? About my past? I am sure I do not know what you mean. One would have to have a past in order for such rumors to exist, Miss Bingley."

"Of course, dear," Caroline purred, her fingers tapping rhythmically against her teacup. "And it is hardly becoming of a governess to engage in idle gossip. However, it seems that certain stories have followed you here to Pemberley, and I would be remiss if I did not express my concern for the reputation of this esteemed household."

My hands clenched into fists beneath the folds of my dress as I struggled to suppress the rising tide of anger and fear within me. What could these rumors be? And did they even exist, or was Caroline Bingley simply inventing them to anger me further?

"Miss Bingley, I assure you that any stories you may have heard are nothing more than idle gossip. I am proud of my conduct thus far in my position at Pemberley, and I can only hope that Mr. Darcy and his cousins share this sentiment."

"I am sure they do," Caroline said, her eyes narrowed in cruel satisfaction. "But one cannot help but wonder how long your good fortune will last, especially considering the... colorful nature of these tales."

"Colorful nature?" I echoed, my anxiety mounting. "I am afraid I must insist upon knowing the particulars of these rumors, Miss Bingley. If they are truly so scandalous, I must defend myself against them."

"Ah, but Miss Bennet," Caroline replied with a smirk, "I am certain you know as well as I do that the mere mention of such things would be most improper in polite company. It is far better for us to let sleeping dogs lie, as they say."

"Is that so? Well then, if you will not tell me what these rumors are, I must assume that they are merely the product of idle minds and overactive imaginations."

"Assume what you will, Miss Bennet," Caroline said, her grin widening at the sight of my discomfort. "But remember this: even the smallest hint of scandal can cast a long shadow upon one's reputation."

I struggled to maintain my dignity in the face of such provocation.

"I am confident that my conduct has always been above reproach, Miss Bingley."

"Confidence can be a double-edged sword, Miss Bennet," Caroline replied coolly, a cruel smile playing on her lips. "One never knows what whispers might be circulating behind closed doors. And once a rumor takes hold, it can be impossible to dispel."

At that moment, I heard the sound of the front door opening, followed by the familiar voice of my dear Aunt Gardiner. Overwhelmed with relief at her arrival at Pemberley, I excused myself from Caroline's horrid presence and hurried to greet her.

"Elizabeth!" Aunt Gardiner exclaimed upon seeing me, pulling me into a warm embrace. She had always been such a source of comfort in my life, and I was grateful for her presence now more than ever.

"Welcome to Pemberley, Aunt Gardiner," I said, forcing a smile. "Let me show you to your room."

As I led her upstairs, Aunt Gardiner marveled at the opulence of the estate. "My dear niece, what a magnificent home you have found yourself in!"

"It most certainly is," I replied, my voice tight with emotion. "It is a place of great beauty and refinement."

Upon reaching her room, I opened the door to reveal an elegantly appointed chamber, complete with a roaring fire and a view of the snow-covered gardens outside. My aunt expressed her delight at the accommodations, but I could not shake the feeling of unease that had settled upon me since my conversation with Caroline.

"Is something the matter, dear Lizzy?" Aunt Gardiner asked gently, detecting my distress.

"Oh, Aunt Gardiner... Caroline Bingley has intimated that there are rumors circulating about me," I confessed, my voice barely above a whisper. "Rumors that could jeopardize my position here at Pemberley."

"Rumors?" Aunt Gardiner's brow furrowed in concern. "What kind of rumors? And how would Miss Bingley be privy to such information?"

"I do not know. But her words have struck fear into my heart, and I cannot help but worry for my future here."

Aunt Gardiner's eyes held a warm understanding as she squeezed my hands reassuringly. "Come, sit with me by the fire, and let us talk of this further," she suggested.

I allowed her to lead me to the plush settee near the roaring flames, feeling the heat chase away the chill that had settled upon me since Caroline's malicious attack. My aunt sat beside me and rested her hand upon my own.

"Tell me, Elizabeth, what exactly did Miss Bingley say regarding these rumors?"

Drawing a deep breath, I recounted the conversation as best I could, relaying Caroline's snide remarks about my position as a governess and her insinuations about my past. With each word, my anxiety grew, but I forced myself to continue, knowing that my aunt would offer wise counsel.

"Well, It is clear to me that Miss Bingley is acting out of jealousy and spite. She sees your happiness here at Pemberley and wishes to undermine it in any way she can."

"I am sure you are right, Aunt Gardiner," I conceded, though my worry still gnawed at me. "But what if there is some truth to these rumors? What if there is something from my past that I am unaware of, something that could tarnish my reputation?"

"Elizabeth," Aunt Gardiner said firmly, her gaze holding mine, "do not fall prey to Miss Bingley's poisonous words. You must trust in yourself, in your own integrity and goodness. If there is any truth to be found, it will reveal itself in due time. And if there is none, then these rumors shall amount to nothing more than idle gossip."

Her conviction bolstered my spirits, and I felt a spark of defiance ignite within me.

"I shall not allow Caroline Bingley's malicious insinuations to cast a shadow over my happiness."

"Bravo, my dear!" Aunt Gardiner praised, her eyes twinkling. "Now, let us turn our thoughts to happier matters. I have come to Pemberley to enjoy the holiday season, and we shall not be deterred by the likes of Miss Bingley. What say you?"

I smiled at her determination, feeling lighter already.

"Indeed, Aunt. Let us make this a most memorable Christmas!"

Seven

The evening holiday festivities to welcome my Aunt Gardiner to Pemberley had been a delightful affair, with laughter and merriment echoing through the grand halls. However, amidst the light-hearted banter, as well as Caroline Bingley's persistent efforts to charm Mr. Darcy, I could not help but feel an inexplicable tug towards the gentleman.

Even as I tried to dismiss these emotions, they persisted, growing stronger with each passing moment. It was as if some invisible force was drawing me towards him, defying all logic and reason. The more Caroline attempted to drive us apart, the more intrigued I became by his enigmatic presence.

"Fitzwilliam, have you seen my new dress? It is the very latest in fashion!" Caroline gushed, her voice dripping with boastfulness. Her words fell on deaf ears as Mr. Darcy was preoccupied with Joshua and Nicholas, and could not seem to take my eyes off of Darcy.

"Excuse me," I murmured, slipping away from the group and seeking refuge in the quiet sanctuary of Pemberley's vast library. The dimly lit room provided a welcome reprieve from the clamor of the party, and I sighed in relief as I closed the heavy door behind me.

As I perused the seemingly endless rows of books, my fingers gently trailing along their spines, my thoughts drifted to Mr. Darcy. I came to Pemberley looking only for a chance to change my perspective but now I felt as if my whole life were about to change... I just did not know how.

"Miss Bennet?" A deep voice resonated from the shadows, causing me to startle and drop the book I held in my hands. My heart pounded in my chest as I turned to find myself face-to-face with none other than Mr. Darcy himself.

"Mr. Darcy!" I gasped, placing a hand over my racing heart. "You startled me."

"My apologies, Miss Bennet," he replied, stepping further into the candlelight. "I did not mean to frighten you."

"Of course not. I merely sought some peace and quiet away from the festivities. I did not expect to find anyone else here."

"Nor did I," he admitted, his gaze lingering on me for a moment before turning towards the books that lined the walls. "The library has always been a refuge of mine as well."

A silence settled between us, as comfortable as it was unexpected. The tension that had once permeated our interactions seemed to have dissipated, leaving only a sense of familiarity.

"Mr. Darcy," I began hesitantly, curiosity getting the better of me. "Might I inquire what brings you to the library this evening?"

He hesitated for a moment before answering, his countenance softening as he spoke.

"Truth be told, Miss Bennet, I found myself similarly seeking solace from the commotion of the celebration. I have had many things on my mind as of late and thought this would be a quiet place for contemplation."

"Ah, I see," I responded, smiling at the shared sentiment. Despite Caroline's best efforts to drive a wedge between us, I realized then that the attraction I felt towards Mr. Darcy was far stronger than any external force. In that quiet corner of Pemberley, with the sounds of laughter and music fading into the distance, it was as if the universe had conspired to bring us together.

We exchanged glances, our fingers brushing against one another as we reached for the same book. The flickering candle-light danced across the spines of the books, the shadows an audience to this unexpected moment. Our fingers still lingered near the leather-bound volume we had both reached for, and I could feel the heat radiating from Mr. Darcy's hand even though our skin was not touching. The tension between us was palpable, as if the air itself had slowed around us.

"Miss Bennet," Mr. Darcy began hesitantly, his voice barely above a whisper. He paused, taking a deep breath to steady himself before continuing. "I must admit that I find myself in quite the predicament. You see, despite my best efforts, and those of others who shall remain nameless, I cannot deny that I am increasingly drawn to you."

I blinked in surprise at his candid confession, unsure how to respond. Though I had felt a growing attraction towards him, I had never expected him to reveal his own feelings so openly. My heart raced as I considered his words, and I found myself momentarily speechless.

"Mr. Darcy," I managed to stammer out after a moment. "I am quite surprised, sir." My eyes met his, searching for any hint of deceit or insincerity, but all I saw was the depth of his affection, shining brightly within the darkness of his gaze.

"Our chance encounter here in this library has presented me with an opportunity I could not ignore. I have long admired your intelligence, wit, and beauty, but it is your steadfastness in the face of adversity that has captured my heart entirely."

His words sent a shiver down my spine, the sincerity behind them touching me deeply. At that moment, I knew that Mr. Darcy's feelings for me were genuine, and as I looked into his eyes, I could no longer deny the truth to myself.

"Mr. Darcy," I whispered softly, my voice trembling with emotion. "I must admit that your words have left an indelible mark upon my heart."

"Elizabeth," Darcy breathed, a note of reverence in his voice as he uttered my given name for the first time. "You have no idea how much joy your words bring me. My sole intention now is to make you and the children happy, and to prove myself deserving of your regard."

As we stood there, amidst the hallowed tomes of Pemberley's library, a feeling of hope burned within me like the flames of the fire. I knew that the holiday season would not only be filled with laughter and merriment, but also the sweet promise of love and a bond destined to span a lifetime.

Our conversation continued late into the evening. The warmth of the fire crackled in harmony with our laughter as we shared stories of our families' holiday traditions. At that moment, surrounded by the dim light of the library and the warmth of the fire, I knew a profound shift had occurred in our relationship. To think that only a few weeks before, I had viewed Mr. Darcy as arrogant and insufferable. Now, I could not imagine a future without him.

As the fire began to dwindle, we knew it was time to part ways for the night. Reluctantly, we stood and prepared to leave the sanctuary of the library behind. Darcy bent to retrieve his forgotten book from the floor, and as he straightened, our eyes met once more.

"Until tomorrow, Miss Bennet," he said softly, pressing a gentle kiss upon my hand.

"Tomorrow, Mr. Darcy," I replied with a smile, watching him disappear into the shadowy hallway.

With each step toward my bedchamber, a renewed sense of hope blossomed within me. The holiday season, which had seemed so bleak at Longbourn, now promised to be filled with warmth and love. And to think, it was all because of Fitzwilliam Darcy...

Eight

The drawing room at Pemberley was a sight to behold during the Christmas season, with holly and ivy festooning the mantelpiece above a roaring fire. The warmth of the room enveloped me as I entered, and I found myself in the company of Mr. Darcy and Miss Caroline Bingley.

"Ah, Miss Bennet," Darcy greeted me with a nod and a soft smile. "I trust you have been enjoying the festivities thus far?"

"Oh, I have, sir," I replied, butterflies dancing in my stomach when we locked eyes. "Pemberley has never looked lovelier."

"Your presence here certainly adds to the beauty of the estate," he said, and I felt my cheeks flush at his compliment.

Caroline, ever watchful of our exchanges, chimed in with feigned enthusiasm.

"Why yes, Miss Bennet, your arrival has indeed been a breath of fresh air. Though it must be quite the change for someone of your... modest background to experience such grandeur."

"Your concern is touching, Miss Bingley," I replied, choosing to ignore her veiled attempt to belittle me. "Yet I assure you, I adapt well to new surroundings."

"Marvelous!" she exclaimed. "It is a rare quality for one in your position to possess. Tell me, what inspired you to take on the role of governess? Was it perhaps the allure of rubbing shoulders with society's finest or simply the financial necessity?"

"Miss Bingley," I answered calmly, even though her words stung, "my choice to become a governess was made out of a genuine love for teaching and guiding young minds. I find great satisfaction in my chosen vocation."

"Oh, do you? How commendable. And dare I say, it has provided you with unforeseen opportunities as well."

"Opportunities, Miss Bingley?" I asked, feigning innocence.

"Nothing of consequence, I am sure," she replied airily, her eyes flitting between Darcy and me. "Merely a passing observation."

"Speaking of opportunities," I said, deftly shifting the topic away from myself, "I understand that the holiday season is a time for grand events and social gatherings in Lambton. Have you any plans to attend festivities this year, Miss Bingley?"

"Indeed, we do," she replied, her tone as icy as the winter land-scape beyond the window panes. "In fact, Darcy and I shall be attending the annual Yule Ball at Branford Hall tomorrow evening. It is quite the occasion, with guests traveling from far and wide to partake in the seasonal revelry."

"Oh, how delightful," I responded. "Christmas celebrations have always held a special place in my heart. There is something magical about the season."

"Quite so," Darcy agreed, his gaze meeting mine for a moment, before turning to Caroline with a hint of reproach. "However, one must also remember the true spirit of the holidays – goodwill towards others and a generosity of spirit."

Caroline pursed her lips, apparently struggling to maintain her composure in the face of Darcy's veiled reprimand. Her eyes narrowed as she glanced between us once more, clearly sensing the bond between Darcy and me.

"Indeed, Fitzwilliam," she replied, attempting to regain her footing. "And in that spirit of generosity, perhaps it would be fitting to extend an invitation to Miss Bennet to join us at the Yule Ball."

A surge of joy filled me at the prospect of attending such an event, but I swiftly tempered my excitement, not wishing to appear overly eager. "Oh, I could not possibly impose upon your gracious hospitality, Miss Bingley."

"Your company would hardly be an imposition, Miss Bennet," Darcy interjected. "In fact, I believe it would be a most welcome addition to the party."

"Very well, then," Caroline said, forcing a smile that did not quite reach her eyes. "Miss Bennet, consider yourself cordially invited to the Yule Ball at Branford Hall."

"Thank you, Miss Bingley. I shall be honored to attend."

"However," she continued, the air in the room suddenly shifting, "do remember that the ball is a formal affair, and some of the ladies in attendance will undoubtedly don their most exquisite gowns and jewels. You can not wear any old thing, as you are this evening."

"Rest assured, Miss Bingley," I responded, my voice steady and unwavering in spite of my anger, "I have every intention of presenting myself in an appropriate manner for such an esteemed occasion."

Darcy, reaching the limits of his patience with Caroline's relentless insinuations, finally addressed her directly.

"Caroline, enough. Your intentions are transparent, and I must insist that you cease these attempts to undermine Elizabeth. She has more than proven herself as a valued member of this household, and her presence at the ball will only serve to enhance the evening's festivities. You are acting abhorrently."

Caroline stared at him, disbelief etched across her features, before lowering her gaze. "Very well, Fitzwilliam. I apologize to you if she took offense to anything I said."

Darcy stomped his foot on the floor, startling us both.

"That was not an apology, Caroline! Your behavior this

evening has been most unbecoming. Your repeated attempts to disparage Elizabeth in order to advance your own interests are not only transparent but entirely unacceptable. I will not tolerate such conduct toward anyone, least of all of the woman I love."

Caroline's eyes flashed with defiance, and she opened her mouth to retort. But Darcy raised a hand, silencing her before she could utter a word.

"Do not attempt to justify your actions, Caroline. It is futile. The truth is plain to see, and my regard for Elizabeth remains unwavering."

"Very well," Caroline replied icily, her lips pressed into a thin line. "But do remember, Fitzwilliam, that the world will judge you for the company you keep."

"That it will," Darcy responded, his tone measured. "And I am proud to be associated with someone as intelligent, kind, and generous as Elizabeth Bennet."

Caroline's cheeks flushed with anger, and she clenched her fists. However, after a moment of tense silence, she seemed to accept the futility of her actions.

"I shall take my leave of Pemberley then," she announced, her voice dripping with disdain. "It is clear that my presence here is no longer welcome."

"Caroline," Darcy began, his expression softening ever so slightly. "You are correct. Until you can properly apologize to Elizabeth, you are not welcome at Pemberley. I will let your brother know as soon as I am able."

"Very well," Caroline acquiesced reluctantly, her gaze avoiding both Darcy's and mine as she made her way toward the door. "I shall depart for London immediately."

As the heavy oak door closed behind Caroline, I felt relief wash over me. Darcy's unwavering defense of my character had touched me deeply.

"Elizabeth," Darcy said softly, coming to stand beside me once more. "You must know that I meant every word I said to Caroline.

Your presence here at Pemberley has been a source of great joy to me, and I would gladly confront any foe or danger to keep you here with us."

"Thank you, Fitzwilliam," I whispered, my emotions threatening to spill over as I looked into his sincere eyes. "Your support means more to me than words can express."

"Then let us put these unpleasant events behind us," he suggested, offering me a tender smile. "We have much to celebrate during this holiday season, and I cannot think of anyone with whom I would rather share these moments."

"Fitzwilliam, I—" I stammered, my heart racing in my chest.

"Please, let me finish," he said gently, his gaze never leaving mine. "I find myself unable to spend another moment without expressing my desire to take you as my wife. Will you marry me, Elizabeth Bennet?"

His words hung in the air, and for a moment, time seemed to stand still. My mind raced with a thousand thoughts, each fighting for precedence. But all at once, I knew what the answer should be.

"Your declaration has touched me deeply," I replied, my voice barely a whisper. "I confess that I, too, love you with my whole heart and can not wait for you to be my husband."

The warmth of Darcy's grasp enveloped me like a cozy blanket as we stood together in the drawing room. I could feel the tension that had been entwined around our hearts for so long finally dissolve, leaving only the sweetest love behind.

"Shall we join the others for the Christmas celebration?" Darcy asked, his eyes sparkling with anticipation.

"I think we should give them all quite the surprise," I replied. And arm in arm, we made our way to the grand hall where the rest of the family had gathered.

Nine

Christmas Day at Pemberley was nothing short of enchanting, truly putting one in the holiday spirit. Holly boughs and evergreen garlands draped the walls, while wreaths adorned with bright red ribbons graced each door. The light from wreathed chandeliers filled the rooms, and the scent of cinnamon and pine filled the air. The hearth in the grand hall crackled to life with a roaring fire, its warmth radiating throughout the estate, as if to chase away the winter's chill.

As I walked down the hallway on this most delightful of mornings, my heart swelled with anticipation for the day ahead. There was much to look forward to - the presents, the laughter, and, of course, telling our loved ones of our plans.

Upon turning a corner, I nearly collided with Mr. Darcy, who had just emerged from his chambers. For a moment, we both stood still, surprise etched upon our faces. Then, in unison, we broke into matching smiles

"Good morning, Miss Bennet," he said, his voice rich and deep, as if it were a symphony resounding through the halls. "A very Merry Christmas to you."

"Mr. Darcy," I replied, my cheeks warming from more than just the heat of the fire nearby. "Merry Christmas to you as well."

"Let us not tarry," Fitzwilliam said, extending his arm to me. "For our loved ones await, and I dare say they are growing impatient."

"Indeed, we must not keep them waiting," I replied, taking his arm. And as we walked towards the grand parlor, hand in hand, I felt a warmth that had nothing to do with the roaring fire or the festivity of the season. It was a warmth that came from within - from the love I felt for this most unique man.

Upon entering the grand parlor, we found Joseph, Nicholas, and Aunt Gardiner had already arrived, their faces alight with eager anticipation. The room itself was beautifully adorned, with garlands of holly and ivy draped elegantly across the walls. There was a towering Christmas tree in the corner, its branches laden with delicate ornaments and flickering candles. The boys sat around the tree, watching it with excitement until they spotted their cousin and me.

"You are awake, at last!" exclaimed Joseph, rising from the floor to run over to us. "I wanted to wake you up but Nicholas would not let me."

"Indeed, your tardiness had us all quite concerned," Aunt Gardiner chimed in with a teasing smile. "But what better morning to enjoy a long winter's nap!"

"Apologies for our delay," Mr. Darcy replied, avoiding my gaze. "I assure you, we were merely lost in conversation."

"Of course, of course," Aunt Gardiner said, waving away our apologies as she gestured for us to join them. "Now, come, let us begin the festivities!"

We took our seats among our loved ones, and the exchange of gifts commenced. Each present was unwrapped with great excitement and laughter, revealing tokens of love and thoughtfulness that warmed my heart.

Joseph received a fine leather-bound journal for drawings from his Cousin Fitzwilliam, who knew of his passion for sketching birds in the garden. He grinned from ear to ear as he admired the fine craftsmanship, vowing to fill its pages with images of every bird he saw.

Nicholas, who was particularly fond of the horses, was gifted a lovely little wooden horse on wheel that he could pull around behind him when he. played. His eyes shone with delight as he carefully rolled it around the parlor, laughing when they both tipped over their haste.

Aunt Gardiner's face lit up when she opened her present from me - a delicate lace shawl I had spent many evenings working on in secret. She held it up to the light, admiring the intricate patterns and thanking me profusely for such a heartfelt gift.

As each person received their presents, I found my gaze continually drawn to Mr. Darcy. Our eyes met time and again, exchanging knowing smiles and unspoken words of affection. In those moments, I felt the true depth of our connection, and I could not help but be grateful for the affection we shared.

Finally, it was time for Darcy and I to exchange our gifts. With a hint of nervousness, I handed him a small parcel wrapped in brown paper and twine. He carefully unwrapped it to reveal a set of cufflinks engraved with horses, inspired by his love for the animals and his fondness for the stables at Pemberley.

"Elizabeth, these are exquisite," he said, his voice filled with emotion. "Thank you."

"You're most welcome, Fitzwilliam."

He then presented me with a small velvet box, which I opened with trembling fingers. Inside lay a delicate gold locket, encrusted with tiny pearls.

"Fitzwilliam, this is... beautiful," I whispered, unable to tear my eyes away from the precious gift.

"I hoped you might like it," he replied softly, meeting my gaze with an intensity that left me breathless.

After gifts were exchanged, we took our places at the dining table. I could not help but marvel at the sumptuous Christmas breakfast laid out before us. The warm scent of freshly baked bread and crisp bacon wafted through the air, mingling with the sweet aroma of cinnamon and orange from the mulled wine. I glanced over at Darcy, who was seated beside me, his eyes shining with contentment.

"Mr. Darcy," Aunt Gardiner said, "this feast is truly a testament to your excellent taste and hospitality."

"Thank you, Madam," he replied, his cheeks flushing slightly. "But it would be remiss of me not to acknowledge the hard work of our staff in preparing such a splendid repast."

"Indeed," Aunt Gardiner answered, her eyes twinkling merrily. "It almost makes one wish to abandon all propriety and indulge in a bit of gluttony!"

Once plates were emptied and appetites satiated, Darcy cleared his throat, gaining the attention of everyone present.

"If I may have your attention for a moment," he began, his voice steady despite the hint of nerves I detected in the gentle tremble of his hands.

"Of course, Mr. Darcy," Aunt Gardiner replied graciously, curiosity evident in her gaze.

"First, I would like to wish all of you a wonderful Christmas, especially Mrs. Gardiner, who has elected to spend her holiday with us."

"Here, here!" Joseph and Nicholas chorused in agreement, raising their little glasses of milk in a toast.

"Secondly," Fitzwilliam went on, his gaze meeting mine with an intensity that sent shivers down my spine, "I have some news to share. Miss Elizabeth Bennet has done me the great honor of accepting my proposal of marriage."

For a moment, silence reigned as Aunt Gardiner, Joseph, and Nicholas absorbed this unexpected revelation. Then, a cacophony of cheers, congratulations, and well-wishes erupted, filling the room with joyous noise.

"Elizabeth, my dear niece," Aunt Gardiner exclaimed, her eyes glistening with unshed tears, "I am so very happy for you!"

"Thank you," I replied, feeling my own emotions swell within me, threatening to spill over. "I am grateful for this most wonderful Christmas."

As the celebrations continued around us, Mr. Darcy and I locked eyes, our fingers intertwined, causing my heart to beat happily. And I could not help but be grateful for the love that had blossomed between us that most magical of Christmases.

Dreaming of a Pemberley Christmas

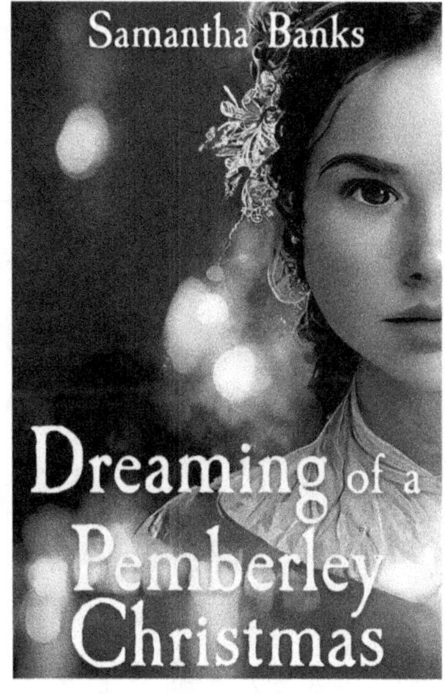

One

This was not the Christmas that Elizabeth Bennet anticipated when she left Longbourn to be with her Aunt and Uncle Gardiner. Ever since she accepted their invitation to spend the holiday with them in Lambton, she had visions of delicious feasts, warm fires, and cheery carols around her aunt's piano. Instead, she now found herself lost in a sudden snow storm, shivering from head to toe, with no hope of rescue in sight. And it was her fault alone that she was in this ridiculous situation.

Elizabeth and the Gardiners were spending December in the home of a distant cousin who recently moved to America. While he was abroad, their cousin requested that various family members tend to his house and property in his absence, and the Gardiners chose to do so in December so they could enjoy a proper country Christmas. And since Jane had gone to Brighton with their younger sisters for the winter, it seemed the perfect time for Elizabeth to take time away from Longbourn.

They were not in Lambton long, however, before it began to snow. It snowed every day, sometimes very little, and sometimes a lot. But it did not take long for Elizabeth to feel as if she were going mad. Eventually, the morning came when it did not matter what dangers awaited her... she needed a breath of fresh air, regardless of the consequences.

"Lizzy," Aunt Gardiner said as she handed her niece her mittens, hat, and scarf. "Perhaps it would be best if you simply open the window and take a deep breath that way."

"No, Aunt. I need fresh air, and I intend to get it, come what may."

"Please, Lizzy. Do not play the fool," said her uncle. "It can do no good to wander around the countryside when no one can get to you. You will only catch your death of cold."

"I appreciate your concern, Uncle, but remember, we are not entirely isolated here. We are not far from town. Should I get in any trouble, someone is bound to come around who can help me."

Her aunt tried in vain several more times to stop Elizabeth from leaving the house, but if she did not stretch her legs or see the sky, she was not sure she would make it to Christmas morning.

When she first left the house, all was well. The sky was clear and while it was cold, the fresh air was bracing after so much time cooped up inside. But it was not long before dark gray clouds rolled in and it suddenly began to snow once more.

Elizabeth wondered if she might find her way back to the house, but it was impossible to see a thing, and she inadvertently took a turn onto the steeper part of the lane that led in the other direction. As soon as she took a step, she slipped on a patch of ice and began to slide. She grabbed at branches and bushes as she went, and it felt as if she might roll down the hillside, but at last she managed to catch herself.

She looked back up the hill and saw that she was close to a tiny house she did not see before. Elizabeth crawled to her feet and began walking, trying to avoid becoming so breathless that she would fall again. She had not walked far when she began to feel the first twinges of pain in her side from where she strained to pull her legs free of the snow. And it was not long before she was wiping the snow from her lashes.

The little house was closer at last, but there was no smoke billowing from the chimney, which meant no one could be inside. It was far too cold for anyone to be home without a fire burning. Elizabeth looked around. There was no other house, no barn, and no animals. She began to wish she never left the comfort of the house she shared with her aunt and uncle.

Elizabeth knocked on the door and waited for someone to answer. It was so cold. Even if someone opened the door, she would be too weak to speak. She coughed, hoping to attract attention. But there was no one home. The house was completely dark inside. It was as if no one had lived there for years. Finally, with no other options and the cold paining her down to her bones, Elizabeth ignored propriety and opened the door to the small forest cabin...

And she could not believe what she saw inside.

Two

When the bright light illuminating off the snow lit the dark cabin, Elizabeth was shocked to see three children huddling together in the corner. They were dressed in rags and their faces red from the cold.

"What in the world are you doing in here?" Elizabeth asked them over the sound of the wind. When she could not tolerate the cold any longer, she stepped inside the cabin and forced the door shut. It was considerably darker, but at least she could hear herself think.

One of the children, a girl who looked to be around eight, turned to Elizabeth and said, "Our father left us here."

"Goodness! What is your name?"

"I am Amelia," she said. "This is my brother Caleb, and this is my sister, Hannah."

"How long have you been here?" Elizabeth asked.

"We do not know. But it was snowing when our father brought us here."

That did not mean much. It had been snowing since Elizabeth arrived in Lambton.

"Where is he now?"

The children all shrugged.

"He went away," the littlest one, Hannah, said. Elizabeth turned to the oldest, Caleb.

"Do you know when he will be back?"

He shook his head, but Amelia answered.

"Caleb can not hear, nor does he speak. Father said only that we would be safe here, and someone would find us eventually. But it feels as if it has been so long..."

The little girl's voice trailed off, but Elizabeth could still see the sadness in her eyes. How could someone just leave these children alone in the middle of a snow storm with no heat or food?

"Where is your mother?" Elizabeth asked.

Hannah shrugged and Amelia looked to the ground.

"She ran away one night. She took nothing but the clothes on her back and left us with father."

Elizabeth could not believe what she was hearing. How could anyone abandon children like this?

Amelia, who still had not looked up from the floor, mumbled, "The door was locked from the outside. From the tree."

"What?" Elizabeth asked, crouching on the floor so she could see their faces. "What do you mean?"

"He locked the door and blocked it so we could not get out. At least, that is how it was the last time we tried. Then the snow was too heavy and it was not safe to leave."

With a sigh of frustration, Elizabeth stood and looked out the window. The snow was still falling heavily, and it did not look like it would be stopping any time soon, but one thing was for certain...

She would not leave these children alone in this dreadful cabin. There had to be something she could do.

It was only then that she noticed chimney smoke billowing up into the clouds just through the woods. Elizabeth could not be sure exactly how far away the house was, but anything was better than freezing in this cabin. And the children clearly needed to eat. She turned back to them and knelt down on the floor.

"I have an idea, little ones. Are you willing to trust me?"

Three

This was not the Christmas holiday that Fitzwilliam Darcy expected. When his sister Georgiana wrote to him and informed him that she would remain in Brighton for the winter, he did not wish to sully her good humor by letting her know how disappointed he was. This was to be his first Christmas free of his obligation to Anne de Bourgh, now that she eloped with her piano tutor. Darcy intended to throw a lavish holiday celebration to mark the occasion of his freedom, but with Georgiana away, there seemed little point.

It was a cold, snowy afternoon, yet again, when Fitzwilliam told the majority of his staff they could return to their families for Christmas. There was no need for the entire household to have their holiday ruined as well. Only his housekeeper, Mrs. Reynolds, and butler, Mr. Martin remained. While he was grateful for their company and their loyalty, he could not help but feel a bit guilty that they would all be wandering around Pemberley alone on this most joyous of seasons.

Darcy spent the rest of the day in his study, absorbed in his work and, in particular, the estate ledgers. His steward had been keeping them up to date for some time, but Darcy found he had a new appreciation for the fruits of their efforts, given how much work there was to be done. The day passed by quickly and, before Darcy knew it, it was dark outside, and colder still.

Darcy locked up his study and went in search of some supper. He hoped Mrs. Reynolds had not gone out of her way in preparing a meal, but there was no doubt that he had built up a tremendous appetite at his work. Just as he passed the front door, however, he was surprised by a furious knock. He looked at the clock in the hall and saw it was after six.

"Who in the world could be out in this weather?" he asked aloud as he made his way to the door. Darcy almost dropped the glass of port in his hand when he opened it and saw Elizabeth Bennet on his front step, with three young, shivering, emaciated children by her side.

"Miss Bennet!" he said, surprised. "What are you doing here?"

"Perhaps I could tell you the story inside," she replied.

He did not want to leave them outside for any longer than necessary, so Darcy invited them all in the house at once. He led them toward the parlor, where he knew the fire was lit and there were comfortable chairs for the children to sit in.

"We are so sorry to impose upon you in such a way, but I fear it was an emergency," Elizabeth said.

The youngest girl was whimpering, and Darcy, without hesitation, took off his jacket and wrapped it around her shoulders. Then he hurried back to the foyer and called out to his housekeeper.

"Mr. Martin! We need all the blankets you can find! Mrs. Reynolds, a tray of tea and biscuits for four people at once!"

While his staff carried out his orders, Darcy took a moment to assess the situation. As he suspected, the children appeared to be most frightened. Now that they were sitting by the fire, they sat still and quiet, but Darcy could see the tension in their shoulders.

Seeing the children's state, he knelt down next to Elizabeth and said, "Perhaps you should tell me what is going on."

"These children are Amelia, Caleb, and Hannah," she said, pointing to each of them. "Their father left them in a small cabin in the woods on your property several days ago at least. I was lost in the snow storm and happened upon them. It was sheer luck that I discovered them at all."

Darcy closed his eyes. He could not believe what he was hearing. What kind of a man would do something so cruel? And how could he have possibly left them in this condition? Darcy looked up and saw Mrs. Reynolds had just brought the tray of tea and biscuits. He helped her set everything on a table next to Elizabeth and the children.

"Please, help yourself," Mrs. Reynolds said. "I shall be at the kitchen door if you need me. Sir, may I speak to you for a moment?"

Darcy followed his housekeeper to the foyer because he could see the concern in her eyes. Once they were alone, she turned to him with her eyes wide.

"Mr. Darcy, sir, those children need more than tea and biscuits. They need to see a doctor. They need clean, warm clothes, a bath, and a hearty meal. You can not simply give them some tea and send them back out into the snow... sir."

He smiled at Mrs. Reynolds and patted her on the shoulder. "Of course not, dear lady. Of course not. I am sure some of Georgiana's old things will fit the girls. And the boy can have anything of mine that will be useful. Whatever they want to eat, make sure it is done. It seems we will have visitors in the house for Christmas after all..."

Four

Elizabeth watched as Mr. Darcy and two of his staff members hurried around the house without saying anything to any of them. When they walked through the trees and into the clearing, the sun long gone and the cold brutal, she should have been elated to see the massive estate before them. But when she realized it was Pemberley, Elizabeth felt nothing but fear. Her last encounter with Fitzwilliam Darcy was less than pleasant and she could not be sure he would even open the door for them, let alone welcome them into his home.

It was quite the surprise, then, when he let them in with hardly a question. Now, the children were on their third pot of tea, second tray of biscuits, and draped in the finest blankets Elizabeth had ever seen. After a short conversation with Mr. Darcy, the housekeeper departed for the kitchen, and Darcy asked Elizabeth to join him in the library.

"Excuse us for the moment, children," Elizabeth said. Darcy watched as the older girl seemed to communicate with the boy using her hands. Then the children nodded and continued to munch on the treats. Once they were alone in the library, Darcy turned to Elizabeth with a polite smile.

"Do you need anything else, Miss Bennet? Are you warm enough?"

Elizabeth pulled the heavy shawl Mrs. Reynolds gave her tighter around her shoulders.

"I am much better now, thank you. I can not express how grateful I am that you have taken us in for the night. Tomorrow morning, we can try to make our way to town so we will not trouble you further. I need to find their family... somehow."

Darcy shook his head adamantly.

"I will not hear of it. It is far too dangerous for anyone walk in this snow, let alone the children. The girl is so little and the boy?"

Elizabeth sighed.

"He can not hear and does not speak. But they communicate with each other quite well. Mr. Darcy, please excuse my frankness, but what kind of father abandons their children in a cabin with no food or warmth? Not a stitch against the cold? I do not believe in violence but in this case..."

Darcy nodded.

"You do not need to finish, but I agree with you. Which is why I refuse to turn you or those young children back out into the snow. You will all stay here until the storm subsides. Is there someone who will worry about you?"

She nodded.

"My Uncle and Aunt Gardiner are going to be worried senseless. I feel terrible about leaving but had I not, Amelia, Hannah and Caleb would still be alone in that terrible cabin."

"We will find a way to get word to them as soon as it is safe to do so. In the meantime, I would like you and the children to change into warm, clean clothing and then join me for a proper meal. I am sure you would all like to eat something more than tea and biscuits."

Elizabeth smiled at him with gratitude and was amazed when he returned her smile with one of his own. Not the polite, distant smile he usually gave to strangers, but a warm, friendly smile that made Elizabeth feel at ease in his presence.

After changing into a nice dress and a warm shawl, Elizabeth felt much better. Once she was done, she helped Mrs. Reynolds dress and wash the girls, and ensure Caleb had everything he needed. When the children saw the rooms where they would be sleeping, their eyes lit up in surprise. Hannah picked up a small wooden doll in a pale pink dress, and Mrs. Reynolds only nodded.

"Miss Georgiana has no need for dolls anymore. I am sure she would be very happy to let you have that, Hannah."

The little girl's smile warmed the last bit of cold in Elizabeth's bones.

Five

When they joined Darcy in the dining room, Elizabeth was surprised to find he and the butler had laid out a fantastic meal for her and the children. There was a beautiful roasted goose with potatoes, green vegetables, bread and butter, and even a cake for dessert. Elizabeth watched as all the color returned to the little ones' cheeks in an instant. They looked to Darcy for permission to sit and the moment he waved his hand, all three of them charged directly to the table. No one said a word as they devoured everything put on their plates and asked for more. It was only when the kids had their fill that Elizabeth and Darcy began to take food for themselves.

"We are so grateful for your charity and kindness, Mr. Darcy," Elizabeth said, as Hannah and Amelia nodded in agreement. Amelia gestured to Caleb and he turned to Fitzwilliam to nod a thank you as well.

"No, do not say another word about it. I'm afraid I have more questions than I do answers, but I am glad you brought them here. I could not in good conscience leave you out in the snow. And certainly not on the day before Christmas Eve."

Elizabeth took a long sip of wine and relished the taste of it.

She would never again take food or drink for granted, especially after all those poor children had endured.

"Mr. Darcy, you have heard all there is to hear of my story. The only story left to hear is the children's," Elizabeth said as she tried to politely cut her goose, though she wished to eat all of it in one bite.

Amelia, who was rosy cheeked and smiling from filling her belly, told Fitzwilliam everything she said to Elizabeth in the cabin. Though she added one detail Elizabeth could not have anticipated. She told him about a man who had come to the cabin, with a red cloak and green eyes. She said he was terribly scary and watched them through the cabin window.

"Do you know who he was?" Darcy asked. Elizabeth shook her head, having never heard of such a man. Then Darcy turned to Amelia.

"And you do not know what happened to your father, Amelia?"

The little girl's eyes filled with tears and she began to cry. Hannah took her napkin from the table and handed it to Amelia to wipe away her tears. Darcy felt a stab of heartbreak at the sweet gesture between the little sisters. He did not wish to pressure Amelia to speak any further, nor did he wish to upset the children more.

"This discussion can wait until tomorrow, I think. For now, we shall eat cake in front of the fire and talk of Christmas! Would you like that?"

All three children smiled with delight and pushed their chairs back to gather around the fireplace. Elizabeth watched them, bright and happy and warm, and realized they could not have happened upon a better host. This family needed love and Christmas spirit, and much to her surprise, Darcy was the perfect person to show it to them.

Before they could join the children in the parlor, Elizabeth was surprised when Fitzwilliam took her hand and stopped her in the foyer.

"Miss Bennet, once the children have gone to bed, would you be willing to speak with me in the library? I would like to discuss their situation further but I do not wish to upset them."

She glanced at Amelia, Hannah, and Caleb as they contentedly ate their cake by the fire. Caleb even cut some of his piece in half and gave more to his sisters. Elizabeth was sure he had tended to their needs for many years, even before they had been left on their own. It made her heart ache.

"Of course, I will speak with you. Sadly, I think there is much more to discover about these children, more than even they know."

"Miss Elizabeth," Hannah called out in her small voice. "Come eat cake!"

Darcy waved for Elizabeth to walk in front of him.

"Let us eat cake, Miss Elizabeth," he said with a smile.

Once the children were tucked away in their beds and fast asleep, Elizabeth crept down the stairs and made her way to the library. Darcy was sitting in front of a roaring fire, sipping tea and reading a substantial book. While everyone at Pemberley had gone to great lengths to keep Elizabeth and the children warm, she could not seem to rid herself of the feeling of being buried beneath a pile of snow. The moment she saw the beautiful fire in the fireplace, she hurried over and began to warm her hands in front of it.

"Would you like me to find you a blanket? Or perhaps a warm coat?" Darcy asked as he set down his book. Elizabeth shook her head.

"The fire is good enough, thank you. I feel I must thank you again, on my behalf and on behalf of the children. If you had not taken us in, I am sure we would have died in that snow storm."

"I am only glad I was here," he said softly.

A comfortable silence fell over them. The fire crackled and Elizabeth felt the heat from it begin to warm her. She was shocked when she felt Darcy's hand on her shoulder. She looked at him, and then he pointed to the grate in front of them. The kettle was on, making the most glorious sound.

"Tea?" he asked.

She smiled and nodded. He retrieved the tea and poured her a cup, then poured himself a cup. Slowly, he handed her the cup and put the teapot on a small table beside them. Then he took his seat again.

"Miss Bennet, what do you think Amelia meant about the man in the red cloak with the green eyes? Was she referring to her father?"

Elizabeth had put much thought into who Amelia might have seen outside the cabin and the only thing she was sure of was that it was *not* their father. But who it might actually be?

"I truly do not know. But the children were without food for days, and only had snow to melt to drink. There is a chance she was seeing things that were not there. I do not know how those poor lambs survived on their own."

Darcy sighed as he imagined how scared they must have been, cold and alone, with no idea when they might be rescued. It was all terrible.

"When the weather clears, I will ask my cousin to look into the matter of the children's welfare. He is a barrister in Lambton and he might have access to information about the children's family. We need to know who abandoned them and why. I wish to be able to help them if I can."

Elizabeth smiled as she sipped her tea.

"Thank you, Mr. Darcy. That is most kind of you."

Another comfortable silence descended between them. Darcy took advantage of it to observe Elizabeth as she sipped her tea and stared into the fire. He wanted to study her as he would a land-scape, to just absorb the view and take in every detail he could. She was beautiful. Her hair was pulled away from her face into a simple plait, and her eyes were bright and lively. She wore the simplest of dresses and the plainest of shoes, but she seemed radiant to him. Her voice was soft, like velvet.

"Mr. Darcy, you are staring at me," Elizabeth said, surprising Fitzwilliam from his reverie. He only had a moment to come up with a proper excuse to explain why he had been doing so.

"Apologies. It appears I am more tired than I realized. Perhaps we should retire for the evening and continue this discussion tomorrow?"

Elizabeth nodded. "I am quite tired. It has been a very long day and I feel as if I could sleep until next Christmas."

Darcy laughed as he helped Miss Bennet to her feet.

"I shall hope against hope to see you in the morning just the same."

When they parted ways at the top of the stairs, Darcy could not help but feel a touch of Christmas joy that Elizabeth Bennet and these children had arrived on his doorstep. Now, he just had to be sure that stayed safe in his company for the rest of their time at Pemberley...

Seven

When Elizabeth woke the next morning, the first thing she did was check on the children to see if they had gone to breakfast. She was shocked to discover them still contentedly sleeping, even though it was well past nine. The little ones looked as if they had not slept in ages and were making up for all of the time they had lost. Elizabeth did not wish to disturb them, so she quietly shut their doors, then went to her room to dress and prepare for the day.

Once she was done, it did not take long for her to discover Darcy, sitting at the dining room table. He was surrounded by scones, fresh fruit, jam and cream, and eggs. Elizabeth realized at once that she was starving. She hurried over to take her seat beside him and wasted no time in reaching for a plate and piling it with food.

"Good morning, Mr. Darcy," she said with a smile as she took a bite of a scone. "Thank you for this. I am famished."

"Good morning, Miss Bennet." He set his newspaper down to speak to her. "One of our stablehands endeavored to ride into town early this morning, so I sent him with a letter to deliver to my cousin. I have asked him to begin a search for the children's father, but I do not hold out much hope that he will be found at this late stage."

Elizabeth had thought the same thing and she paused before she went back to eating her breakfast. Could they hope to find the father of the children? And would they be able to persuade him to take the children back? She was not sure he was even fit to care for them if they *did* manage to find the man again

"I understand." Elizabeth took a bite of egg, then continued. "After hearing their story, I could not bear to see them go to an orphanage or, worse, be sent to live on the streets."

"I thought the same, and thus I asked my cousin to inquire about the matter. I hope he will write to me swiftly with his findings. Though I hope you will not be disappointed if there is no information to be had."

"Of course," Elizabeth said as she scooped some more eggs onto her plate and took a bite.

She glanced up to catch Darcy staring at her, and quickly took another bite. He was still watching her when she was done. She swallowed her food and took a sip of tea.

"Is there something you wish to ask me, Mr. Darcy?"

He put his own cup down and nodded. "In fact, there is. Why were you out walking alone in the snow in a place you do not know well two days before Christmas? It seems rather dangerous, does it not?"

Elizabeth laughed.

"I suppose it does seem rather silly. But I had simply been so confined since we came to Lambton. I had not had a chance to venture out and explore, or breathe fresh air. I was so determined to do it before the holiday that I took the chance to do so on my own. Perhaps it was dangerous, but I would not have found the children had I stayed home."

Darcy smiled as he moved his chair closer to hers.

"Then I am happy you took the risk, but please do not let it happen again. I want to be certain you are safe."

"I will try my best to remember that," she said, then took a bite of another scone before continuing. "What did you do with your morning?"

Darcy picked his newspaper back up and started to read the news.

"I went to my study to go over my accounts. I had planned to finish last evening but it seems I was distracted."

Elizabeth dabbed at the corners of her mouth with her napkin and tried to hide her smile. "I am sorry, of course, that we interfered with your business. And on Christmas! How horrible."

Darcy detected the humor in her voice and could not hide his laughter.

"Noted, Miss Bennet. Perhaps I will let my business matters idle until after the holiday. Are there any activities that you think the children would enjoy? It has been some time since I had to entertain a child."

Elizabeth laughed as she stood to go check on the children once again. It was getting late and they were going to be extremely hungry if they slept much longer. She did not wish for them to wake up with empty bellies.

"First, let us prepare them for the day. Then, we can ask them what they wish to do. They had a very trying time in that cabin and might want to rest. I will bring them down when they are ready. Could you send Mrs. Reynolds to assist me?"

Darcy nodded. "Of course. Right away."

As she left the dining room, he could not help but notice how kind and loving Elizabeth Bennet was toward the children. She hardly knew them and yet she was caring for them as if they were her own. This was a side of her he had never seen before...

And he found it terribly endearing.

Eight

Once Amelia, Hannah, and Caleb were dressed, Elizabeth gathered them together to join Darcy downstairs. But before they could reach the stairs, Amelia took Elizabeth's hand.

"Miss Elizabeth, we have never had clothes as fine as these before, or slept in beds so soft and warm. Even if we must go away today, we are so grateful for everything you and Mr. Darcy have given us."

Amelia threw her arms around Elizabeth's waist, causing tears to well in her eyes.

"Sweet little girl, why would you go away? While I can not say what will be in the future, until this storm passes, none of you are going anywhere. And we will not let you leave until we are sure you are going somewhere safe and sound. For now, Pemberley is all our home. I do not want you to worry for the rest of your time here, understand?"

"Yes, Miss Elizabeth," Amelia said as she wiped a tear from her eye.

"Now, why don't we go see if we can find some breakfast in the kitchen?"

Amelia nodded and they made their way down the stairs. Darcy was still in the dining room when they entered. He looked up and smiled, and he got to his feet as they approached.

"Good morning," he said as he took Hannah's hand and kissed it. "May I have the honor of escorting you to the kitchen?"

"Thank you, Mr. Darcy, sir," she said with a grin. "I would be most grateful."

After helping the children with their breakfast, they all gathered in the library, where Mrs. Reynolds and Mr. Martin were hanging garland and holly on the fireplace mantle. The entire room was decorated for Christmas, and the fire was burning in the fireplace, filling the room with a warm glow.

"What do you think?" Elizabeth asked the children as they stood back and looked around in wonder.

"I think it is wonderful," Amelia said. "We have never seen such lovely Christmas decorations!"

Darcy turned to Caleb, who ran his fingers across the soft needles of the pine garland. Fitzwilliam looked the teenage boy directly in the eyes and spoke slowly and clearly, so Caleb could see every word.

"Do you like it as well, Caleb?"

The boy nodded, then turned to Amelia and signed, allowing her to translate.

"Caleb says it is wonderful and to thank you for your kindness."

"How were you both able to learn sign language? Did your parents teach you?"

Amelia shook her head and smiled sadly.

"Our parents did not teach us anything. When we lived in Leicester, a young minister at the church taught us both. We would stay after services every Sunday until mother left. Then father made us move to Lambton. But we do well enough, right, Caleb?"

Her brother nodded as Mrs. Reynolds returned with a tray of

drinking chocolate, biscuits, and little peppermint candies. All three of the children's eyes went wide at the sight of the rich, delicious cups of chocolate.

"Forgive me," Mrs. Reynolds said as she handed the cups to the children. "I could not seem to find any tea, so Mr. Martin suggested we make some chocolate for you to drink." She gave the adults a conspiratorial smile that the children did not see.

Caleb took his cup and gave it a sniff.

"Smells delicious, doesn't it?" she asked as she took her own cup.

He nodded and took a sip, clearly enjoying the beverage.

Darcy and Elizabeth joined him on the sofa and they all drank in contented silence, enjoying the unique flavors.

After a few minutes, Elizabeth turned to Darcy. "It seems to me we need to come up with some activities for the children. We can not just let them sit around the house all day, can we?"

Darcy laughed.

"No, we certainly can not have that. I am sure they have more energy and excitement than we do. Since the weather outside is still dreadful, perhaps we could tell ghost stories or sing carols? Would Caleb enjoy that at all?"

Amelia nodded. "Very much, sir. He can feel the music as it is played. It was always his favorite part of church."

"I like ghost stories!" Hannah said excitedly.

Elizabeth picked up the smallest child and set her in her lap, giving her a hug. "Then it seems we have a full Christmas Eve ahead of us. Let us get started before we waste any more time!"

Nine

After hours spent telling stories, playing games, and eating every treat that Mrs. Reynolds could make for them, Amelia, Caleb, and Hannah all dozed off in front of the fire just as the sun began to set. They still had some time before their Christmas Eve dinner would be served, so neither Elizabeth nor Darcy wished to wake the children. Especially when they still seemed so tired after their terrible ordeal. Fitzwilliam covered each child with a blanket, tucked a cushion under their heads, and then gestured for Elizabeth to follow him out of the parlor.

Once they were in the library, they were able to speak freely and discuss the small gifts they found around Pemberley to give each of the children.

"Are you quite sure Georgiana will not mind if we give her things to Amelia and Hannah?" Elizabeth asked as she tied a ribbon around the neck of a wooden horse on wheels for the littlest girl. For Amelia, they found a pretty little doll in a pink dress and small silver locket. Caleb was to receive a handsome gold pocket watch that Elizabeth gasped when she saw. Darcy anticipated the question she was going to ask him.

"Georgiana will not mind, and neither do I. The Darcy family has been blessed beyond measure. We have more than we could need in three lifetimes and the very least we can do is share our good fortune with these children. I only wish I could do more."

Elizabeth glanced in the direction of the parlor and felt her stomach twist at the thought of the children leaving. She could not bear the idea of them being sent away to an uncertain future.

"Do you think we will ever see them again, Darcy?" she asked as she looked up at him. "If your cousin locates their father, or if they are destined for some other fate, when the storm passes and Christmas is over, will the children depart from our lives forever?"

Darcy returned her gaze with an equally intense look.

"I am not certain. But I hope that we will cross paths again, and I pray that their future will be filled with love and happiness."

"As do I," she whispered as she turned away to hide the tears. "Oh, what a sentimental pair we are! Let us control our emotions before the children wake and we have to explain ourselves."

Fitzwilliam was overwhelmed by the sudden urge to take Elizabeth in his arms and comfort her, but he restrained himself, for fear he would make her uncomfortable. Instead, he cleared his throat and tucked the pocket watch for Caleb into his coat pocket.

"Shall we go back and sit with them?" Elizabeth asked as she dried her eyes.

"Yes, let's," he said with a smile. "I am sure they will be quite alarmed if they wake and find us not there."

When they opened the door to the parlor, they found the children still sleeping. As it was almost time for supper, they began to gently wake them from their slumber.

"Amelia," Elizabeth whispered softly as she caressed the little girl's hair. "Amelia, sweetheart, wake up."

The child's eyes opened, and she looked around the room in confusion at the unfamiliar surroundings. Then she looked to Elizabeth, and her eyes filled with tears.

"No!" she cried, clasping Elizabeth's hand tightly. "I want to stay with you!"

Darcy and Elizabeth looked at one another in confusion.

"Amelia, love, you are not going anywhere," Darcy said as Hannah woke and crawled into his lap. "No one is going anywhere, except to the dining room for a delicious feast! You are all safe. Now, dry your tears and let us enjoy our Christmas Eve roast, for we still have a wonderful evening ahead."

Elizabeth gave Amelia a hug as Caleb took his sister's hand to lead her to the dining room. Whatever nightmare plagued the little girl seemed to have passed, but Elizabeth could not help but feel worried about the future. What would happen if they *did* try to take the children away?

And was that something Elizabeth even wanted?

After a delicious feast of roast beef, turnips, fresh bread, and a beautiful Christmas pudding, the entire household gathered around the fire in the sitting room to sing carols. Before they could begin, however, Elizabeth and Darcy surprised the children with their gifts.

Caleb's eyes grew wide with interest as he turned the watch over in his hand. He signed a grateful thank you to Darcy before sitting down to examine the time piece. Hannah ran her horse in circles around the sitting room while Amelia played joyously with her new doll. The locket Darcy gave her sparkled in the firelight. As the children played, and Darcy sipped a glass of port, Elizabeth could not help but feel immense joy. And she never wanted it to end.

Once they had finished their carols, Darcy instructed the children to go upstairs to bed so they would be awake in time for Christmas breakfast. They did not need to be told twice, and within moments of leaving the sitting room, they had disappeared up the staircase. Darcy and Elizabeth looked at one another, and she felt a peculiar fluttering in her chest.

Darcy smiled and pulled her into his arms. He kissed her until she lost her breath, her sense of reason, and her awareness of everything around her. When he finally stopped, she felt dizzy and utterly surprised.

"What was that for?" Elizabeth asked as she tried to catch her breath.

Darcy smiled. "Because I love you."

Elizabeth's heart leapt. "You do?"

"It would seem I do, Elizabeth. I am in love with you. I have always been. It likely comes as a surprise, but I have had a great affection for you for some time. Spending this time with you, and the children, has only confirmed what I was sure of once upon a time."

"But what if we had never happened upon each other again?" she asked with a smile. "Why did you never tell me?"

Darcy laughed and kissed her again.

"I was meant to marry my cousin Anne. This had been the plan since we were children. But as I spent more time with your sister and Charles, I began to realize that I could not spend the rest of my life with a woman who I did not care for the way I cared for you. I never laughed with Anne. I never thought about her the way I do you, and the idea of spending the rest of our lives together made me quite miserable. And then, like a miracle, when you arrived on my front step, I decided that I must seize my own happiness."

"And do you think that you and I can be happy together?"

He smiled and took her hand in his.

"I know so."

Elizabeth rested her head against his chest and sighed. "I believe you mean that, but it is still hard to believe you remember what you loved about me after all this time."

Darcy leaned back and took her face gently in his hands.

"I love you, Elizabeth. I love the way you made merry in a Pemberley winter. I love the way you turn thoughtful when you are lost in your poetry. I love your wit, your intelligence, your sense of humor. I love the way your eyes sparkle when you surprise me with one of your silly arguments, and I love that you risked your life to save these children. You are an extraordinary woman, Miss Bennet."

Darcy paused, waiting for Elizabeth to speak, but she was too overcome to do so. Instead, she smiled, and kissed him again.

"Merry Christmas to you, Mr. Darcy."

"Merry Christmas to you, Miss Bennet."

Darcy led her over to the fire. They sat on the rug in front of the fire as it hissed and popped. Darcy told her stories about his childhood Christmases, and she told him about her sisters and their adventures. It was not long before the clock struck midnight, and the pair welcomed Christmas together as two people who had received the most unexpected gift of all...

Love.

Eleven

The next morning, Elizabeth was roused from her bed by the sound of little feet running down the hallway. She had only just put on her robe when there was a tiny knock on her door. When she opened it, she discovered Hannah on the other side.

"Sweet buns, Miss Elizabeth?" she asked, holding up the doll she had been given the day before. Elizabeth put on her dressing gown and slippers, then scooped Hannah off the floor.

"Let us go see if Christmas breakfast is ready, little one!"

Elizabeth carried Hannah to the dining room and sat her at the table. They were the first to arrive, but the fire was already crackling in the fireplace. Hannah grabbed a muffin from the basket on the table, and examined it carefully. Then she looked up at Elizabeth with her eyes wide, and smiled.

"Can I have sugar in my tea?" she asked hesitantly.

"Of course, you can!" Elizabeth laughed. She poured herself a cup, and then fixed one for Hannah. The little girl took tea cup happily and then blew on it to cool it down before wrapping her hands around it.

"Thank you, Miss Elizabeth," Hannah said softly.

Elizabeth smiled and nodded.

"I hope you enjoy your Christmas breakfast."

Darcy and the rest of the children soon arrived, and they all sat down to a sumptuous Christmas breakfast of eggs, ham, toast, muffins, and even honeyed Christmas bread. Elizabeth loved watching the children enjoy their food. They all asked for seconds, even Hannah. As the children ran off to fetch their Christmas treasures, Elizabeth and Darcy took seats by the fire, and he poured them each another cup of tea.

"It was a lovely Christmas morning, was it not?" Darcy said as he took her hand.

"I have enjoyed every moment," Elizabeth said. "And I think the children have, too."

Darcy squeezed her hand. "I am glad."

"And I think," Elizabeth said quietly, "that we shall enjoy many more moments together as well."

Fitzwilliam turned to her and looked her deeply in the eyes.

"Elizabeth, I did not sleep a wink last night thinking about this very thing. If the children have been abandoned, they will need a home, a family. And perhaps..."

Darcy was interrupted by a sudden knock on the front door. He looked at the clock and was surprised to see it was only ten.

"Who could be here this early on Christmas morning?" Elizabeth asked as they stood up and walked to the foyer. When Darcy opened the door, he was shocked to see his cousin, Bernard Heathfield, standing in the cold. His top hat was covered in a thick layer of snow, he was shivering, and even his mustache had small ice crystals within it. Fitzwilliam quickly ushered him inside of Pemberley's warm walls.

"Bernard, what in the world are you doing here? You should be home with your wife, not out in this terrible snow."

Darcy shut the door and led his cousin to the hearth. He

poured Bernard a glass of brandy and had him drink it down. When he finished, Bernard sat back in his chair and sighed.

"I am sorry to interrupt your Christmas morning but I am here for the children, Fitzwilliam. I came to take the children back to Lambton."

Twelve

❧

Elizabeth turned to Darcy in a panic.

"Fitzwilliam... we can not let them go. We can not! Mr. Heathfield, are you saying that you located the children's father?"

Bernard took off his hat and set it by the fire, then refilled his brandy before speaking.

"I did not, though after speaking with our constable, I was able to ascertain his identity. The children are Caleb, Amelia, and Hannah Radcliffe. Their mother, Letty, took up with some artist and left the children with their father, Theodore. This Teddy fellow is apparently quite the scoundrel and left the girls with the boy, who suffers from some sort of..."

Darcy held up a hand. "He is deaf. But capable of communicating."

Bernard shrugged as if this was all a formality.

"Yes, well. The constable was not surprised when I showed him your letter. He was surprised at the manner of the abandonment, which was reprehensible of course, but not the abandonment itself. Regardless, I suspected you would be ready for the children to be out of your hands, so I am going to take them to the church tonight. Tomorrow, they will go to an orphanage... elsewhere. Miss Bennet, if you wish to return with me, the main roads are clearer once you get further from Pemberley."

Elizabeth's whole face crumpled at the thought of the children, so filled with joy and love and safety, being taken from Pemberley and put in a cold, unfeeling orphanage. She pulled on Fitzwilliam's sleeve.

"You are not going to allow these children to leave, are you?"

Darcy turned to her and took her hands in his. He looked into her eyes, and then said quietly, "Elizabeth, they are not our children. We do not even know if they want to stay here."

"But how can you say that?" she cried. "You have seen their affection for you, for us. We have seen the changes in them, even after such a short time. Pemberley is healing them. Please, do not give up on them."

Darcy looked at her and saw that her cheeks were wet with tears. Her eyes glistened like the frosty winter trees outside. This was certainly not how he imagined starting a family, though he did have to admit that the children had been happy at Pemberley. Could this be what he had been looking for all along?

"Bernard," Darcy said as he approached his cousin. "If the father can not be located, would it be possible for the children to stay here? At Pemberley?"

Bernard looked at him, astounded. "You want the children to stay?"

Darcy turned away from his cousin and walked to the fireplace, then turned back to him.

"Yes. I want the children to stay."

The barrister appeared confused.

"I do not understand. You are an unmarried man. Certainly, you do not plan to raise these children by yourself?"

Elizabeth walked to the fireplace and stood next to Fitzwilliam, and he smiled as he took her hand.

"Cousin Heathfield, I would like you to be the first to know that Miss Bennet and I intend to be married."

Bernard looked from Elizabeth to Darcy, then back to Elizabeth in shock.

"Well, this is quite a surprise. Congratulations, indeed! I suppose that if you are to marry Miss Bennet, it is perfectly reasonable that the children stay. It is preferable to spending Christmas lighting candles at the church."

Darcy clapped his cousin on the shoulder.

"Brilliant, Bernard. And you can obtain the constable's consent for the children to remain here?"

Bernard thought for a moment, then nodded. "I do not see why not. I suppose I will return to Lambton and let you get back to your holiday. Merry Christmas, one and all."

Elizabeth touched Darcy's arm and smiled.

"A merry Christmas, indeed."

Thirteen

No sooner had Cousin Bernard departed Pemberley than the children returned from their rooms with their Christmas presents. Elizabeth and Darcy allowed them to play and read and make merry for some time before giving them what they hoped would be the good news.

"Children," Elizabeth said. "Mr. Darcy's cousin, Mr. Bernard Heathfield, was just here. And he had some very interesting information for us all."

After Amelia translated for Caleb, all three children looked at her with anticipation painted on their faces.

"The first bit of news is that Mr. Darcy has asked me to marry him, and I have accepted his offer."

The children cheered and clapped for the couple, and little Hannah even gave Darcy a hug. Elizabeth could not help but notice his cheeks turn rosy from happiness.

"What could be better news than that?" Amelia asked.

"Well," Darcy said, "we would like for all three of you to stay here with us, at Pemberley, for as long as you would like. Until your father returns, of course."

The children looked at each other and then back to the couple.

Caleb said something to Amelia, which she spoke aloud to Darcy and Elizabeth.

"Caleb asked, does this mean we can stay here forever? We do not have to go to the orphanage?"

Elizabeth felt tears well in her eyes.

"No, you do not have to go to the orphanage. We promise."

The children cheered and hugged Elizabeth and Darcy. Elizabeth hugged them back and felt a happiness like she had never imagined.

"You will not have to go to the orphanage," Elizabeth said, her voice muffled by Caleb's hair. "We are a family now."

The children cheered again, and Mrs. Reynolds appeared at the door, clapping her hands at seeing all the happiness.

Darcy clasped Elizabeth's hand and whispered,

"A family. I like the sound of that."

AFTER A WONDERFUL DAY spent playing games, singing carols, and eating until they were stuffed, it was finally time for Christmas to come to a close. They settled the children in their rooms, and then Elizabeth and Darcy retired to their own chambers. Elizabeth could not believe that soon, she would begin married life with a man she loved and the children who had touched her heart.

"Are you happy, my love?" Darcy asked as they walked arm in arm toward their rooms.

"Happy? I am overjoyed. I never imagined I could be so happy."

Elizabeth glanced up at Darcy with a smile on her face. Her cheeks glowed with happiness, and her eyes sparkled with joy. "I cannot believe I am going to be your wife."

"I cannot believe you are going to be my wife, either."

After they kissed goodnight and parted ways, Elizabeth curled up under the covers in her warm, beautiful bed. She watched as a light snow began to fall outside, coating everything in a fresh white powder. They would likely be stuck inside for another day or more if it snowed for very long. But for the first time since Elizabeth Bennet arrived in Lambton...

She did not mind at all.

Her Christmas Suitor

The holiday season had descended upon Longbourn, and the Bennet family found themselves surrounded by the joyful chaos that accompanied it. The kitchen bustled with activity as Mrs. Bennet and her daughters debated what sumptuous meal to prepare for Christmas dinner. Elizabeth stood in the midst of the commotion, her eyes sparkling with merriment as she added another suggestion to the already lengthy list.

"Roast goose would make a fine addition, do you not think?" she offered, grinning at her sisters.

"Indeed, it would," chimed in Lydia, clapping her hands excitedly. "And perhaps a fine plum pudding?"

"Absolutely!" agreed Jane, her smile lighting up her face.

As the sisters continued their culinary debate, Mrs. Hill, their housekeeper, entered the room with an elegant envelope in her hand.

"Miss Elizabeth, a very fancy messenger has just arrived with this for you."

Elizabeth's heart skipped a beat as she eyed the exquisite handwriting upon the envelope. She reached for it with trembling fingers, suddenly feeling the weight of expectation bearing down upon her.

"An invitation, Lizzy?" asked Jane curiously, trying to catch a glimpse of the contents. "Could it be for an event in the new year? It is awfully late to invite you to anything now."

"Let us see," Elizabeth whispered, tearing open the envelope with bated breath. Her eyes widened as she read the words on the invitation – a Christmas ball at Netherfield, hosted by its newest tenant, Charles Bingley! As the reality of the event began to dawn upon her, a mixture of excitement and nerves took hold of her. How would she fare in such esteemed company?

"Jane, it appears we have been invited to a Christmas ball at Netherfield!" she exclaimed, unable to contain herself any longer. A chorus of gasps filled the room, followed by a flurry of excited chatter.

"Good gracious, a ball? At Netherfield?" cried Mrs. Bennet, clasping her hands together in delight. "We have heard nothing but gossip about Mr. Bingley since he arrived in Meryton, yet we have not seen him once! And to invite you to a holiday ball? He must think us truly important."

"Will you look at that!" Mr. Bennet chuckled, peering over Elizabeth's shoulder. "A chance for my daughters to mingle with high society."

Before further discussion could take place, the door burst open. Elizabeth's best friend, Charlotte Lucas, charged toward her without standing on ceremony.

"Lizzy, I have news!" she cried, waving her own invitation in the air.

"Charlotte! We have just received invitations to a Christmas ball at Netherfield," Elizabeth informed her, matching her friend's excitement. "You must be attending as well!"

"Oh yes, I am!" replied Charlotte, her cheeks flushed with anticipation. "And what's more, I have heard that the two most eligible bachelors in the country, Mr. Fitzwilliam Darcy and Mr. Joseph Watkins, are expected to attend!"

"Mr. Darcy and Mr. Watkins? Truly?" Elizabeth felt a surprising thrill at the prospect of meeting both gentlemen, and she pondered whether Christmas magic had a hand in this serendipitous turn of events. Her heart raced as visions of elegant dances and witty conversations filled her mind.

"Then we must prepare ourselves for a truly unforgettable evening," said Elizabeth, linking arms with Charlotte as they joined the others in excited chatter about the upcoming event.

The promise of romance, laughter, and holiday enchantment now hung in the air like the sweet scent of fresh pine and gingerbread, and Elizabeth could not help but believe that this would be a Christmas to remember.

Kitty, her eyes wide with anticipation, turned to Elizabeth and tugged on her sleeve.

"Surely, the invitation includes all of us?"

"Alas, Kitty," replied Elizabeth with an apologetic smile, "the invitation is only for Jane and myself."

Upon hearing this, the younger Bennet sisters could not help but pout, their excitement quickly turning to envy. However, Mrs. Bennet, ever the determined mother, seized the moment to direct her attention to her two eldest daughters.

"Jane, Lizzy, you must go and pick out your finest Christmas attire for the ball! My daughters shall be the best dressed there if it kills me!"

Mr. Bennet, overhearing his wife's proclamation from across the room, raised his eyebrows and added dryly, "And it very well might if Jane and Elizabeth do not put on a good showing."

Elizabeth could not help but feel a pang of sympathy for her father, who was often caught in the whirlwind of her mother's schemes. She glanced at him, her eyes sparkling with amusement.

"Fear not, Papa. We shall endeavor to do our utmost to ensure that the evening is nothing short of extraordinary. This will truly be an exciting Christmas for us all."

As Elizabeth and Jane made their way upstairs to peruse their gowns, with Charlotte close behind, they could hear the soft murmur of their sisters' grumblings below. In the sanctity of their shared bedchamber, the sisters rifled through their garments in search of the perfect dresses to wear, with Charlotte to provide her opinion on their choices.

"Look at this one, Lizzy, Charlotte," Jane said, holding up a gown of deep green silk with delicate gold embroidery. "Do you think it would suit me?"

"Oh, yes," said Charlotte. "The color looks lovely on you."

"Indeed, it would, Jane," Elizabeth agreed, her gaze lingering on the exquisite fabric. "And I believe I shall wear this one," she said, selecting a gown of rich burgundy adorned with intricate ivory lace.

"Ah, that is a lovely choice, Lizzy," Jane said with a smile.

As they prepared their outfits, thoughts of the upcoming ball and the possibility of meeting Mr. Darcy and Mr. Watkins swirled through Elizabeth's mind. She wondered what kind of men they were and whether they would live up to the expectations society had placed upon them. Would they be as charming and witty as they were reported to be? Or would their wealth and status have made them cold and unapproachable?

"Come, Jane," Elizabeth murmured, rousing herself from her reverie. "We must make our plans for the morrow – for we have much to do before the ball."

Together, the sisters laid out their gowns and accessories, chatting with Charlotte all the while about the excitement and anticipation for the magical evening to come. And Elizabeth knew in her heart that, whatever happened, it would be a Christmas they would never forget.

Elizabeth stepped into the ballroom at Netherfield, her eyes wide with amazement. She wore a rich burgundy gown that suited her perfectly, the fabric shimmering under the soft glow of countless candles. Her sister Jane was by her side, looking every bit the beauty in an emerald gown that made her hazel eyes sparkle. Charlotte, their dear friend, was equally stunning, clad in deep royal blue that contrasted wonderfully with her dark curls.

"Good heavens," Elizabeth murmured, unable to tear her eyes away from the quests and exquisite decorations. Garlands of holly and ivy adorned the walls, and the air was filled with the scent of cinnamon and pine. A massive fir tree, dressed in glittering ornaments, stood proudly near the grand staircase, while twinkling crystals hung above them, casting a delicate light over the room.

"Simply breathtaking, is it not?" said Jane, leaning in to speak quietly to Elizabeth.

"It most certainly is," Elizabeth replied, her gaze traveling across the room, taking in the elegantly attired guests as they chatted and laughed together.

"Ah, there you are, my dears!" Lady Stoppard cried out to

them. Their mother's friend's voice carried easily over the din of conversation as she approached. "I have someone I would like you both to meet!"

She beckoned to a gentleman who stood nearby. As he turned to face them, Elizabeth could not help but notice his striking features: strong jaw, high cheekbones, and sparkling blue eyes that seemed to dance with mirth. His wavy chestnut hair was impeccably styled, and his tailored suit accentuated his tall and broad-shouldered frame.

"Miss Elizabeth, Miss Jane, may I introduce Mr. Joseph Watkins?" Lady Stoppard gestured grandly to the handsome man before them. "Mr. Watkins, these are the lovely Bennet sisters."

"Charmed, I am sure," Joseph said with a warm smile, taking each of their hands in turn and bowing gracefully.

"Mr. Watkins is quite a lively gentleman," Lady Stoppard confided in a stage whisper, earning a good-natured chuckle from Joseph. "He told me the most wonderful joke earlier. He will have to tell you as well."

"Is that so?" Elizabeth replied, her curiosity piqued. She had not expected Mr. Watkins to be such an all-together intriguing character.

"Miss Elizabeth," Joseph began, his eyes twinkling mischievously, "might I have the honor of your first dance this evening?"

"Me?" Elizabeth asked, genuinely surprised. She had never been one to attract much attention from potential suitors, particularly when compared to her beautiful sister Jane.

"Of course," he affirmed. "If you would do me the great pleasure?"

"Of course," Elizabeth agreed, feeling a flush rise to her cheeks. She glanced over at Jane, who beamed delightedly at her sister's good fortune.

"Miss Bennet, I trust you shall not be left without a partner for long," Joseph winked conspiratorially at her, and she giggled softly.

"Thank you, Mr. Watkins," Jane replied, her cheeks pink with pleasure. "I am certain that will not be the case."

As they made their way toward the dance floor, Elizabeth could not help but feel a flutter of excitement in her chest. The night was off to a promising start, and she could hardly wait to see what other surprises awaited.

THE SUMPTUOUS SCENTS of cinnamon and cloves filled Elizabeth's senses as she weaved through the crowded ballroom, parched from the dance and scanning the room for the elusive punch bowl. She had barely taken two steps when she nearly collided with a familiar figure clad in deep royal blue.

"Charlotte!" Elizabeth exclaimed, steadying herself. "Where have you been hiding?"

"Right here, Lizzy," Charlotte laughed, her eyes sparkling merrily. "But I must say that our collision was most fortunate, for it appears I have an introduction to make."

Elizabeth followed her friend's gaze to a tall gentleman standing nearby. He was a strikingly handsome man, his dark hair curling slightly at the temples. His deep brown eyes studied the room and appeared to find it less than pleasing. His demeanor was reserved, but there was an unmistakable air of mystery about him.

"Miss Elizabeth Bennet," Charlotte began, gesturing toward the gentleman, "may I present Mr. Fitzwilliam Darcy?"

"Mr. Darcy, it is a pleasure to make your acquaintance," Elizabeth said, curtsying politely.

"Likewise, Miss Bennet," he replied, bowing gracefully. Though his voice was guarded, it held a touch of warmth.

"Miss Bennet," Mr. Darcy continued, "I hope I am not too bold in requesting the honor of your first dance this evening."

"Alas, Mr. Darcy," Elizabeth responded, trying to hide her surprise at being asked by such a distinguished gentleman, "I have already given my first dance to Mr. Watkins. However, I would be delighted to offer you my second dance, if it pleases you."

"Very well," he conceded, a hint of disappointment flickering in his eyes. "It shall have to suffice. You may find me whenever you wish, Miss Bennet."

With a nod, Mr. Darcy disappeared back into the throng of guests.

"Good heavens, Lizzy!" Charlotte gasped, her eyes wide with astonishment. "Two dances with such distinguished gentlemen? You have truly been bestowed with a Christmas gift!"

"Charlotte, please," Elizabeth implored, feeling her cheeks redden. "Do not tease me so. I have never danced with such esteemed company before, and I am anxious not to cause my mother any embarrassment."

"Simply enjoy yourself, my dear friend. Just mind your steps, lest you inadvertently crush these fine gentlemen's toes."

"Your counsel is always invaluable, Charlotte," Elizabeth replied, rolling her eyes good-naturedly. She longed to tell her friend that her advice was not terribly helpful, but before she could do so, she found herself being swept away by the bustling crowd.

With a sigh, Elizabeth resumed her search for the punch bowl. Navigating through the sea of elegantly dressed guests, she could not help but feel a mixture of excitement and trepidation at the prospect of dancing with Mr. Darcy. The evening held the promise of enchantment, but only if she could manage to keep her nerves - and her footsteps - in check.

$$\mathcal{T}hree$$

The soft flicker of candlelight danced off the polished floors as Elizabeth Bennet found herself, quite unexpectedly, alone with Mr. Darcy in a quieter corner of the ballroom. The lilting tune of a waltz floated through the air, providing a gentle backdrop for their conversation.

"Miss Bennet, I must say that I find your love for literature quite refreshing," Darcy began, his voice tinged with sincerity. "I do enjoy reading myself, especially during the winter months when the nights are long and quiet."

"Is that so, Mr. Darcy?" Elizabeth replied. "There is something magical about curling up with a good book by the fireplace, particularly during the Christmas season."

Darcy inclined his head in agreement.

"It provides an escape from the hustle and bustle of holiday preparations. I find it a most welcome respite."

"True," Elizabeth mused, feeling a growing connection with the man before her. "This holiday has a way of bringing out the best in people, even in the midst of the most trying circumstances."

Their conversation was cut short, much to her temporary

disappointment, as the waltz ended and the next dance began. Darcy extended his hand towards Elizabeth, his eyes imploring.

"May I have the pleasure of this dance, Miss Bennet?"

"Of course, Mr. Darcy," she replied, placing her hand in his with a warm smile.

As they joined the other couples on the dance floor, a small string quartet struck up a lively rendition of "Deck the Halls." Elizabeth's spirits lifted at the sound of the familiar tune, and she could not help but share her enthusiasm.

"I simply adore Christmas carols, Mr. Darcy! They fill the heart with such joy and warm memories."

"Yes, I suppose," Darcy replied, a hint of amusement in his tone. "While I can appreciate the sentiment behind them, I must confess that I prefer the more somber songs of the season."

Elizabeth's brow furrowed, and she was about to voice her annoyance at his dismissal of her opinion when Darcy continued.

"However, I can see the appeal of the more lively tunes, as they do provide a delightful accompaniment for dancing."

His admission, coupled with the genuine smile gracing his lips, charmed Elizabeth in a way she found most unexpected. She looked upon Mr. Darcy in a new light, as someone who could appreciate the simple joys of life, even if he held a preference for more serious pursuits.

"Yes, there is something to be said for the way these melodies bring people together, encouraging them to set aside their differences and embrace the spirit of the season."

As they danced, Elizabeth marveled at the ease of their conversation. The music and the joy of the surrounding company filled her heart with a happiness she had not realized she had been longing for. And perhaps, just perhaps, she thought as she met Mr. Darcy's eyes once more, there might be more than just friendship blossoming between them on this magical Christmas evening.

As the lively notes of "Deck the Halls" faded, the couples on the dance floor shared their final bows and curtsies. Mr. Darcy bowed gracefully to Elizabeth, his eyes lingering on her face for a moment before he spoke.

"Miss Bennet, might I have the pleasure of another dance later in the evening?"

"Of course, sir," Elizabeth replied with a smile that made her cheeks warm. With another nod, she left his side and went off to find her sister in the crowd.

After a brief search, she found Jane engaged in conversation with Charles Bingley near the grand fireplace that adorned one wall of the ballroom. The flickering light of the flames illuminated their contented faces as they chatted animatedly, clearly enjoying each other's company.

"Jane, I apologize for interrupting," Elizabeth said, approaching the couple with an air of hesitance. "But may I speak with you for a moment?"

"Of course, Lizzy," Jane replied, her own radiant smile never leaving her face as she turned to address her sister. Charles Bingley, ever the gentleman, excused himself with a polite bow, granting the sisters privacy.

"Jane, you will not believe what has just occurred!" Elizabeth exclaimed, her excitement bubbling over as she relayed the details of her encounter with Mr. Darcy, from their conversation about literature and Christmas magic to their candid exchange about holiday music during their dance.

"Goodness, Lizzy, it seems that Mr. Darcy is quite taken with you," Jane observed thoughtfully once her sister had finished speaking. "And what of Mr. Watkins? You seemed to be fond of him earlier."

Elizabeth sighed, wrinkling her nose slightly in consternation.

"I am fond of Mr. Watkins, but my conversation with Mr. Darcy has given me reason to reconsider my feelings."

"Then I suggest you dance with them both once more, and see which gentleman truly captures your heart," Jane advised gently.

"Would that not only serve to make my problem worse?" Elizabeth mused, her brow furrowing in concern. If she spent more time with the gentlemen, there was a chance she would only grow to care for them both all the more. Still, despite her reservations, she nodded in agreement, knowing her sister's advice was sound.

As the next song began—a lively rendition of "We Wish You a Merry Christmas" that filled the ballroom with exuberance—Elizabeth glanced around the room, her heart pounding in her chest. She spotted Mr. Darcy on one side of the room, his dark eyes meeting hers with a mixture of anticipation and warmth. Across the floor, Mr. Watkins stood as well, his fair hair catching the flickering candlelight as he offered her an inviting smile.

"Go on, Lizzy," Jane encouraged softly, giving her sister's hand a reassuring squeeze. "You must follow your heart."

With a deep breath, Elizabeth took a step forward, her gaze flitting between the two gentlemen. To whom should she go? The answer, she realized with a jolt of clarity, had been clear all along. With newfound determination, she strode gracefully across the polished wooden floor, her heart guiding her steps.

Elizabeth pushed her way through a brilliant sea of red and green dresses as the lively waltz began. Her partner, Mr. Watkins, took her hand with a confident smile and led her into the dance.

"Miss Bennet," Mr. Watkins said, his cool, clear voice easily heard above the music. "I wonder if you know of the architecture of Italy. The home brings it to mind, which is why I mention it. I have been fortunate enough to visit Italy and witness firsthand the grandeur of its buildings first hand."

"Have you?" Elizabeth replied, surprised by his enthusiasm.

"Absolutely! The Pantheon, the Colosseum, St. Peter's Basilica... each more magnificent than the last." Mr. Watkins continued to speak at length about architectural marvels. Throughout the entire conversation, however, he did not once pause to inquire about Elizabeth's interests. Despite his self-absorption, she still found herself captivated by his vivid descriptions.

"Mr. Watkins, you bring these structures to life with your words," she admitted, genuinely impressed.

"I am simply an admirer of beauty, be it in architecture or—" He locked eyes with her, his voice lowering, "—in other forms."

Before Elizabeth could respond, the waltz ended and another began. Suddenly, Mr. Darcy appeared before her, his expression unreadable. He offered his hand, and she hesitated only a moment before placing hers in his. As they danced, the conversation shifted in tone.

"Miss Bennet, I have been told that you possess a charitable nature. Allow me to share with you my efforts during this festive season." Mr. Darcy spoke of the unfortunate families in Lambton whom he aided through provisions and financial assistance.

"Your generosity is commendable, Mr. Darcy," Elizabeth said, studying his face for any sign of insincerity. "And yourself, what interests do you pursue during these celebratory times?"

"Ah, well," he paused, seemingly taken aback by her question. "I enjoy reading and... long walks through the countryside."

"Of course." Elizabeth's mind raced as she tried to discern whether Mr. Darcy's charitable actions stemmed from a genuine desire to help or merely an attempt to impress her and others at the party. His pride and reputation preceded him, but perhaps there was more to him than met the eye.

"Tell me, Miss Bennet," Mr. Darcy said, breaking through her thoughts. "What are your interests?"

"Many things, Mr. Darcy, though I am partial to literature and music." She could not help but compare the two men; while Mr. Watkins had spoken solely of his own passions, Mr. Darcy sought to learn about hers. Still, she could not shake her suspicion that his motives may be less than pure.

The evening progressed, and Elizabeth found herself engaged in more dances with both Mr. Watkins and Mr. Darcy. As she glided across the dance floor, she discovered that each gentleman possessed traits that intrigued her.

"Miss Bennet," said Mr. Watkins, guiding her through a spirited jig, "have you ever traveled to Rome? The architecture there is simply breathtaking." He launched into an animated description of the grandeur of the Pantheon, completely engrossed in his own recollection. Elizabeth listened attentively, appreciating his enthusiasm, though she wished he would exhibit more interest in her thoughts and opinions on anything at all.

"Miss Bennet," said Mr. Darcy during a lively quadrille, "I must inquire about your favorite authors. I am always eager to expand my library."

"I love the poetry of Byron and Shelley," she replied, interested to see if he also enjoyed poetry.

"Ah, both brilliant choices. Their style is unmatched."

As the music paused for a brief interlude, Elizabeth stepped away from the dance floor and found herself drawn to the Christmas tree that dominated one corner of the ballroom. Its branches reached toward the lofty ceiling, adorned with flickering candles nestled amidst sprigs of holly and mistletoe. Delicate wax figurines and blown-glass ornaments danced among the boughs like whimsical sprites, and rustic wooden toys paid homage to the simple joys of childhood.

Pausing near the tree, Elizabeth reflected on the evening's events. Both Mr. Watkins and Mr. Darcy had revealed themselves to be complex individuals, their personalities complementing each other in surprising ways. With Mr. Watkins, she found an undeniable charm and vigor that stirred her curiosity, despite his propensity to focus on himself. In Mr. Darcy, she sensed a well of kindness hidden beneath layers of arrogance and formality, but could not determine if this was genuine or a facade.

Lost in thought, Elizabeth gazed at the twinkling candles and felt the glow of warmth from the holiday season fill her heart. What should she do? The answer eluded her, leaving her with only the gentle rustle of the evergreen branches and the distant laughter of fellow guests to keep her company as she pondered these two captivating gentlemen.

Five

The clock in the hall chimed eleven, its resonant tones echoing through the festively decorated ballroom. Elizabeth could hardly believe that Christmas was but an hour away. She had spent the entire evening dancing with Mr. Darcy and Mr. Watkins, two gentlemen who, to her great astonishment, seemed to appeal to different sides of her own personality.

Mr. Darcy, with his stern countenance and air of importance, challenged her wit and intellect at every turn; while Mr. Watkins, ever amiable and charming, brought out her playful nature and light-hearted spirit. How could she possibly decide which was the better man? Her heart wavered, torn between the two.

As the last dance came to an end, Elizabeth thanked Mr. Watkins and excused herself for a moment. She needed counsel, and she knew just whom to seek.

Elizabeth found Charlotte Lucas standing by the punch bowl, engaged in conversation with a young man she recognized from the militia. With a quick curtsy, she interrupted them.

"Forgive me, Charlotte, but might I have a word with you?"

"Of course, Lizzy," Charlotte replied, excusing herself from the soldier's company.

"Charlotte, I find myself in a most peculiar predicament," Elizabeth confessed, her eyes darting between Mr. Darcy and Mr. Watkins on the other side of the room. "I have spent the evening dancing with both Mr. Darcy and Mr. Watkins, and they each appeal to me in different ways. How can I possibly decide between them?"

"My goodness," Charlotte exclaimed with a surprised smile. "Well, I believe you must follow your heart and embrace the magic of the night. It is Christmas, after all—a season of joy and love. Do not let yourself be torn between the affections of two gentlemen. Rather, listen to what your heart desires most, and allow that to guide you."

"Thank you, Charlotte," Elizabeth said, embracing her friend. "Your counsel, as always, is invaluable."

"Think nothing of it, Lizzy," Charlotte answered with a grin before departing for the crowd. "Now, go and enjoy the rest of the festivities. The night is still young, and anything can happen at Christmas."

Elizabeth, still feeling a flutter of uncertainty in her chest, scanned the room and saw Jane dancing gracefully alongside Charles Bingley. She hesitated for a moment, not wanting to disturb their enchanting waltz, but knew she needed her sister's counsel. Approaching them cautiously, she waited for a pause in the music before extending her hand.

"Jane, might I beg for a moment of your time?"

"Of course, Lizzy," Jane replied with a smile, though her eyes betrayed a hint of annoyance at having to leave Mr. Bingley's side.

"Forgive me for interrupting your dance," Elizabeth whispered apologetically as they stepped aside. "I find myself in a quandary and require your wisdom."

"Whatever is the matter?"

"Both Mr. Darcy and Mr. Watkins have been my partners this evening," Elizabeth began, her voice wavering ever so slightly, "and I cannot discern which man holds greater sway over my affections."

"Ah, dear sister," Jane sighed, glancing back at Mr. Bingley who stood watching them with curiosity. "I am sure you know the right choice, deep within your heart. And as I suspect Charlotte gave you very similar advice, I shall return to my dance. But trust yourself, Lizzy."

"Thank you, Jane, of course."

"Think nothing of it," Jane responded before swiftly returning to Mr. Bingley's arms, eager to resume their dance.

Feeling the weight of both Charlotte and Jane's advice heavy on her shoulders, Elizabeth decided she required a moment of solitude to reflect upon her predicament. She slipped outside, the cold air instantly nipping at her cheeks as she gazed up at the vast expanse of the star-studded sky.

"Dearest heavens," she whispered, her breath visible in the frosty air, "guide me towards my heart's true desire on this wondrous Christmas Eve."

As if in response, a gentle breeze caressed her face, and she felt the stirrings of clarity within her soul. The stars seemed to dance above her, their celestial beauty illuminating the path her heart yearned to follow.

"Mr. Darcy," Elizabeth realized aloud, a surprising warmth blossoming in her chest at the mere thought of his name.

"Miss Bennet?" came a deep voice from behind her, causing her to startle.

"Mr. Darcy!" she exclaimed, turning to face him with wide eyes. "I—I did not hear you approach."

"Forgive me for startling you," he said, his eyes twinkling with mirth. "I came out here for some fresh air and thought I heard you call my name. Did you not?"

"I may have," Elizabeth replied, her cheeks flushed with embarrassment and the cold. "But only because I saw your reflection in a window."

He nodded as if he did not quite believe her response, but then smiled politely just the same.

"May I escort you back inside?" Mr. Darcy offered, extending his arm to her. "It is terribly cold out here."

"Thank you, sir," she accepted graciously, linking her arm through his as they returned together to the warmth of the celebration awaiting them indoors.

Six

The clock chimed midnight, echoing through the grand ballroom and bringing the lively dance to a sudden halt. The anticipatory silence that followed was palpable as guests held their breaths, counting down the seconds until Christmas arrived. Elizabeth Bennet had never experienced such a joyous countdown to Christmas before. And yet, she found herself standing in a moment of trepidation.

On one side of the room, Mr. Darcy stood watching the crowd thoughtfully, as if considering the exercise from all angles. On the other, Mr. Watkins. He was already surrounded by a beautiful group of young ladies, each of them brighter than the candlelight. While Joseph was sure to wave at Elizabeth, she was sure that his attention was hardly focused on her.

"Five... four... three... two... one!" called out the assembled crowd in unison, and then a burst of laughter and cheers erupted around them. The string quartet struck up a joyous Christmas carol, adding to the merriment that filled the room.

After someone cried out that it was snowing, someone pushed open the tall double doors leading to the terrace. They revealed a picturesque scene of freshly falling snow outside. Moonlight flooded into the ballroom, casting an ethereal shimmer over the room and dancing with the warm candlelight.

In that moment, all Elizabeth could see was Mr. Darcy, his dark eyes locked onto hers with an intensity that sent shivers down her spine. It was as though she were seeing him clearly for the first time - not as the brooding, prideful man she had initially believed him to be, but as a person capable of great kindness and love. And in that instant, she knew without a doubt that he was the one.

"Mr. Darcy," she said, taking a step toward him, her voice barely audible above the music and laughter. "Would you perhaps like to look at the snow with me?"

His gaze never leaving hers, he responded with a question of his own.

"Miss Bennet, would you like to look at the snow with me forever?" As he spoke, he reached out and took her hand, sending a thrill through her entire being.

"Forever?" she echoed, her heart pounding in her chest. "What do you mean, sir?"

"Tomorrow," he replied, his voice low and filled with emotion, "I would like to come to Longbourn and celebrate Christmas with your family. And on that occasion, I will ask for your hand in marriage."

A delighted smile spread across Elizabeth's face as she realized the full extent of his intentions. "Mr. Darcy," she whispered, "On that occasion, I will accept."

"Then tonight," he murmured, drawing her closer, "let us just be together, you and I. Let this first Christmas of ours be a memory that we shall cherish for the rest of our lives."

As they stood there, hand in hand, the snow continued to fall gently outside, blanketing the world in a cloak of pristine white. The laughter and music of the ballroom seemed to fade away, leaving only the two of them, lost in each other's eyes and the promise of their future together.

~The End~